The Third Degree

An Eddie Malloy novel

Richard Pitman & Joe McNally

By the same authors

Warned Off
Hunted
Blood Ties
Running Scared
For Your Sins
Bet Your Life

Authors' note

This is a work of fiction. Names, characters, places and incidents are a work of the imagination of the authors or are used fictitiously, and any resemblance to actual persons, living or dead, business establishments, events or locales is entirely coincidental.

ONE

At Newbury racecourse on a bleak November day, Eddie Malloy was legged up into the saddle of a 16-1 chance named Chatscombe. Eddie's previous sixty-two mounts had been losers and, as his toes in paper-thin boots automatically found the cold stirrup irons, he'd already resigned himself to loser sixty-three.

Riders in Eddie's league get used to several winners a week. When that ratio drops, the doubts take hold and savage your confidence and, sometimes, your nerve.

Chatscombe's trainer, George Bloomfield, held his hat on with one hand and slapped Eddie's black-booted leg with his other. 'Good luck! Come back safe!' Eddie rose and gripped the reins, biceps strained by the hard-pulling chestnut as they headed to the start against a rising east wind.

As he pulled up, a rainsquall spattered his flimsy yellow silks. Grimacing, he lowered his head and a barrage of heavy drops echoed inside his crash helmet. He smiled wryly, wondering why he persevered in trying to carve a living from this bone-breaking, dangerous business.

He gathered Chatscombe's reins. The horse pricked his ears and they took their place among the circling horses. The wind sang in the starting tapes. The starter waved them forward. Eddie eased his goggles down.

Chatscombe had spent his career so far as a hurdler; this was his first time over fences. Hurdles are easy to knock down, fences impossible.

A change to bigger jumps can rejuvenate a jaded horse or scare him into a heavy fall. Eddie set off on automatic pilot, pivoting as one with his mount who took the stiff fences in his stride.

Chatscombe's rhythmical gallop and safe jumping nursed Eddie through the first two miles four furlongs in a dreamy state. When the blur of colour materialised into a shouting, waving mass in the grandstands, Eddie found himself in contention, just three lengths adrift of the leader.

Had Eddie been riding winners recently, he would have relished timing his challenge to burst through yards before the finish. But he was a man short on confidence, and went straight for his whip, whacking the surprised Chatscombe down the flanks.

The blow shattered the gelding's concentration and he crashed through the last fence, buckling sideways, bumping his main rival who landed awkwardly.

The natural rhythm Eddie had unwittingly established with Chatscombe was gone. As he scrubbed and kicked, he realized he and the horse were out of synch. But they inched closer to a breathless Bobby Tobin on the sweating, half-winded mare, a neck in front. As they crossed the line, Eddie knew he'd failed by inches to end his bad run.

His sixty-third loser.

Eddie cursed as he pulled up and turned the horse for the exit gate. Tobin, on the winner, cantered alongside, panting and loosening his chinstrap a notch, 'That was hard work!'

'Yeah, you're getting past it,' Eddie said.

'And when did you last ride a winner?'

'When the Pope was an altar boy.'

'Want me to remind you what it feels like?'

'No, thanks. I've got some old videos at home. Maybe I'll watch them tonight.'

'Black and white?'

'Ha bloody ha!'

Tobin, smiling, trotted ahead as they went behind the stands. In the betting ring, Eddie could hear bookies shouting odds on the photo finish, trying to squeeze some extra cash out of the race before the official result was announced. They were offering 5-1 against Chatscombe and no price against Tobin's. An option to bet the loser only. Eddie shook his head; no wonder some bookmakers got themselves bad reputations.

Riding into the bay reserved for the runner-up, he couldn't understand why the result hadn't yet been announced. As he undid the girth and slipped the squeaking saddle off the sweat-stained horse, the PA blared: 'In the third race, the judge has called for a print.'

Eddie and Chatscombe's trainer, looked at each other, then Eddie caught Bobby Tobin's equally quizzical glance. The judge normally asked for a print of the photo finish only when the result was desperately close. A murmur rippled through the crowd. A minute later the announcer's voice silenced everyone: 'Here is the result of the third race: first, number four, Chatscombe; second—'

Even over the noise of the PA, Eddie heard Tobin say, 'You have got to be kidding!'

The print of the photo was put on display, and many more than usual gathered to see that Chatscombe had won by a very short head.

In the changing room, Tobin sat in shell-shocked silence. Eddie patted him on the shoulder then changed into blue and yellow hooped colours and went out to ride in the next.

TWO

His losing sequence broken, Eddie walked into the paddock with more confidence. Halfway across, trainer Matt Nash fell in beside him, slipping an arm around Eddie's shoulders. 'Eddie, I've seen sleight of hand a few times but that's the first time I've seen sleight of head! Well done.'

'Thanks.'

Matt steered him to the centre of the lawn then turned him so they faced each other. The trainer seemed over-excited and nervous. Eddie seldom saw him completely calm; normally Matt fizzed with optimism. Today he was starey-eyed, talking too fast as he gave Eddie instructions on riding Carpathian.

At five nine, Matt stood an inch shorter than Eddie. He'd put on less than half a stone since retiring as a jockey ten years previously, the extra weight taking the gauntness from his frame. Matt was forty-three but kept his brown hair long and unruly, frequently pushing it back from dark, deep-set eyes.

Eddie wore blue and yellow silks, colours he knew were Matt's, which meant Matt owned the horse as well as trained it.

Eddie let the anxious trainer talk himself out, then he looked inquisitively at him and said, 'What the hell's wrong with you? You on speed or something?'

Matt laughed nervously and squeezed Eddie's arm again.

'Nothing like that. I just need a winner. This winner. Be all right then. No problem. Everything'll be fine if— '

Eddie gripped his arm. 'Calm down.' Matt felt the panic rise, bringing a sudden need to pee. He needed to tell Eddie how crucial this was for him, but he didn't want Eddie to feel under pressure. That's when jockeys make mistakes.

The tension eased when a blonde woman in a long camel coat and suede boots with three inch heels joined them. On her coat collar, a diamond brooch brought some glitter to the gloom. The woman's eyebrows were as fair as her hair, which, when Eddie saw it close up, looked to have some darker tendrils among the soft and luxuriant natural blondeness.

Her eyes were a rich hazel dotted randomly with tiny dark specks like black stars. Her skin was pale and smooth. She wore mascara, but no lipstick on her generous mouth. Eddie reckoned she'd be in her mid-twenties and he thought he knew her from somewhere.

She leaned forward, allowing Matt to kiss her and waited to be introduced to the jockey. Matt said, 'Eddie, you remember Rebecca...'

Eddie smiled, holding out his hand. 'I know we've met before, I...'

Rebecca smiled wide showing brilliant white teeth. 'But you're not sure where.'

Eddie still held her hand. She didn't pull it away. 'It'll come back to me.'

'In time for you to ride in this race?'

'Hopefully.' They looked at each other.

Rebecca said, 'I'm Granville Bow's daughter.'

Eddie said, 'Of course. I used to ride for your father years ago! How old would you have been then?'

'Thirteen, fourteen. I remember you much better than you remember me. Had a major crush on you along with half my class at school.'

'No doubt your tastes have improved since then,' Eddie said.

'Don't bet on it,' Rebecca said, and finally let go his hand.

Matt spoke. 'Well, now that you two are reacquainted, I can tell you that Rebecca's got a couple of good horses with me and we're going to win lots of races.' He put his arm around her shoulder and pulled her close, and Eddie wondered if there was more than a trainer/owner relationship there. Matt, as optimistic about his women as his horses, had divorced three times. Rebecca smiled at

Eddie again, eyes glinting. 'Maybe you'll accept my invitation to ride some time?'

Eddie smiled. 'Maybe I will.'

The mounting bell sounded and Carpathian's lad turned the horse onto the lawn. Eddie saw that Matt's nervousness had cranked itself up another notch. They walked toward the big bay gelding. Eddie glanced at Rebecca; the mischief and devilment had gone from her pretty face, replaced by edginess akin to Matt's. Eddie swung into the saddle, wondering what was at stake here.

Watching Eddie canter down the track, Matt blessed himself. He wasn't religious but he needed something to cling to. Superstition would have to do. He had told some very dangerous people that the horse would win at a good price - the main reason he'd booked Eddie to ride. Eddie was a tough guy. He took no shit. Matt admired his riding skills but bugger his riding. Matt needed an ally if things went belly-up. Eddie would make an ideal human shield.

When the suspensory ligament on Carpathian's near foreleg gave way after the fifth hurdle, Matt and Rebecca watched Eddie pull up quickly and dismount. Both lowered their binoculars. Rebecca's head went up, looking to heaven for redemption. Matt's head went down, and he stared into hell.

THREE

Eddie drove to his flat in Shropshire, happy, for once, with a single winner. He'd been disappointed for Matt when Carpathian had broken down. Eddie knew the big horse wouldn't run again.

After the race Matt had seemed shell-shocked, Rebecca Bow dazed, but neither said anything significant to him, so Eddie had expressed his sympathy and left them staring at each other. He had an important dinner that evening.

Dark hair damp from the shower, Eddie stood in his best suit, knotting his tie when the phone rang. He glanced at the clock as he picked up the receiver: 7.50. Matt, still on edge.

'Eddie, you're riding at Taunton tomorrow?'

'That's right.'

'Listen, I've got three runners there.'

Eddie looked anxiously at his watch. 'Sorry, Matt, I'm already booked in ...'

'No, no, no, I don't want you to ride for me, not at Taunton. I wondered if you'd like to leave home a bit earlier and drop in here for the second lot?'

Riding out for Matt would mean getting up before five. He'd been hoping to have a relaxed dinner and a drink. 'Matt, listen, I...'

'I'd like you to ride work on Prince Simba.'

Prince Simba. Matt's stable star, so precious to the trainer that he'd sweated and worked to regain fitness and reapply for his jockey's licence to ride the horse himself. Prince Simba had already won two of the biggest races that season and, whatever Matt's reasons, Eddie would have been foolish to reject this chance.

'Okay, Matt, I'll be there.'

'Good. And I thought that maybe we'd travel to Taunton together.'

'Sure, why not?'

'Don't be late then, will you?'

'I'll be there around eight.'

'That's fine.'

Although keen to get away, Eddie felt obliged to ask about Carpathian. Matt sighed. 'He's in bad shape but who knows, maybe we can do something after a year's rest.'

Eddie smiled. That seemed more like the old Matt; never say die. Eddie went to the mirror to finish this tie-work. He looked at himself and wondered what lay behind Matt's invitation to ride Prince Simba. Why hadn't he mentioned it at Newbury that afternoon?

He slid the knot to the top button of the white shirt and leaned closer to the mirror. His fine-boned face glowed from the hot shower, the one inch crescent scar on his cheekbone raised and pink. Eddie couldn't decide whether to be proud of that scar or not. A few jocks had them, mostly from spills on the track. Eddie got his when a man bit him as he lay trussed up in the boot of a car.

He stood straight and buttoned his jacket, ready for the short walk across the yard to Charles's house. A chef had been brought in; Eddie believed he could already smell the succulence of cooking meat floating on the evening air. He'd been fasting more often lately. His last decent meal a vague memory.

As he was leaving, the phone rang again. 'Eddie, how you doing?' Ken MacAdam, a jockey

'Not bad, Ken, but I'm under pressure, I'm afraid, been summoned by the big boss. You know how it is.'

'Yeah, know it well. Old Indian saying: "He who pays retainer has jockey by bollocks."'

'Not quite as bad as that, but I've got to put in an appearance in about two minutes.'

'No worries. I thought you'd want to hear about this, thinking of your interest in all things mysterious.'

'I'm listening.'

'That winner you rode today, well that so-called winner?'

'Uhuh?'

'The same thing happened to me at Stratford two weeks ago. I got beat a head, maybe more. Took the horse into second spot then bugger me if they don't announce me as the winner! I'll tell you summat, Eddie, I make as many mistakes as the next fool riding horses for a living, but I wasn't wrong that day. That horse did not win that race. Okay, I took my percentage and I banked my present, you've got to go with the flow, but I rode a loser and I know it.'

Eddie had been involved in enough scrapes to recognize the faintest ping of alarm bells. Ken's tale made him uneasy, but he didn't have time to discuss things. 'We're the wrong side of thirty now, Ken. Maybe we should get our eyes tested.'

'The wife says I've got eyes like a shit house rat.'

'Well, it could be we've gone so long without a winner we don't believe it when we get one.'

'You're making me think now, Eddie.'

'Look, mate, I need to go. I appreciate the call.'

'No worries. You at Taunton tomorrow?'

'Yep.'

'See you there.'

'See you.'

Eddie switched on the answer-phone and made a final check of his slim frame in the mirror. He skipped downstairs and hurried across the yard toward the big house, his steps echoing off the cobbles, out into the winter night.

FOUR

Rising in the darkness of a chilly morning and hurriedly pulling on jodhpurs and a warm sweater, Eddie brewed coffee and reflected happily on his dinner last night with Charles Tunney and Eddie's main employer, Broga Cates.

Broga owned the training stables and the surrounding estate. He retained Eddie to ride for him, and Charles Tunney to train his string of twenty-two horses. Broga also owned the flat Eddie lived in on the top floor of a converted barn, overlooking the yard.

Last night the multi-millionaire owner had declared himself in the market for ten more horses. He told a surprised and delighted Charles his budget stretched to £500,000. That could buy four or five decent types, which might carry Eddie to a dozen more wins a season.

Eddie sipped black coffee and reached to touch wood at the thought that yesterday's winner promised a turn of luck. Ten minutes later, he was speeding south to Lambourn to fulfil his promise to Matt Nash.

Matt laboured in the lower ranks of the training profession. Many thought him a fool whose optimism had long ago boiled over into delusion.

They said Matt proclaimed talent in every animal he handled just in case he ever turned out to be right. Eddie, quick to recognize a fellow underdog, liked Matt and rode for him whenever bookings allowed.

At 7.56am, Eddie steered his blue Audi into Matt's driveway and parked close to the house. The front door looked freshly painted in a searing lemon gloss, which reflected the bright morning sun into Eddie's narrowed eyes.

He knocked and turned the handle: locked. Surprised, he stepped back, then hammered with the heel of his hand. 'Come on, Matt, you lazy sod. Get up!'

In black jodhpurs, ankle length boots and a yellow sweater, Eddie stood swinging his riding helmet and whip. If he'd been a couple of paces to his left, he'd have seen the edge of the curtain move behind the kitchen window. A few seconds later, the door opened.

Matt stood, white-faced, wiping his mouth with a tea towel. He too wore jodhpurs, and his ankle boots were of black rubber. A blue open neck polo shirt showed bushy chest hair. As the tea towel swung, it revealed vomit stains on the front of the shirt.

'What's wrong?' Eddie asked.

Dazed and silent Matt tottered backward, opening the door slowly wider. Eddie went up the two stone stairs and into the kitchen. Matt closed the door and locked it.

Out of the sunlight now, Eddie saw Matt's ghostlike pallor. He took him by the arm and sat him on a bench close to the sink. Vomit blocked the plug-hole. Dishes and cutlery lay askew on the white worktop. Shattered glass glittered like a galaxy on the night-black floor tiles.

Eddie filled a mug with water. Matt drank. Eddie watched the faraway look in his dark eyes as the trainer raised his head, wild hair tumbling aside as he emptied the glass.

Matt wiped his mouth and tried to smile. 'Sorry, Eddie. Slight unexpected contretemps with some of my creditors. Was just throwing up when you knocked. Excuse the mess.'

Eddie said, 'Who? What happened? Did they beat you up?'

'Only mentally. Have…have a look in the living room.'

Eddie swung his legs clear of the bench and walked through the open door. Although he lived alone, Matt liked style, and expensive furniture. Eddie surveyed the room. Patches of blood had been daubed on the pale yellow walls and on the hide-covered sofa and chairs. Three of the four rugs on the polished floorboards were blood-stained. The severed head of Matt's King Charles spaniel,

Jinty, lay against the leg of the coffee table, empty eyes fixed on Eddie.

Jinty's body, battered and wrung free of blood, hung from the pale blue shade of the standard lamp in the corner. Eddie returned to the kitchen. Matt, tears rising, looked at him. Eddie put a hand on his shoulder then sat opposite him. 'Have you called the police?'

Matt shook his head slowly and dabbed at the first tear.

'Why not?'

Matt shrugged helplessly, like a child, sounding like one too as he stifled sobs, trying to speak.

'Matt. Tell me what happened.'

FIVE

Matt and Eddie trotted out a few minutes after 8.30, heading for the ancient chalk downland a hundred feet above. Matt sat on 15.2 hands of neat brown gelding, making Prince Simba look huge.

Matt looked skyward. 'Listen to the larks.'

'Never mind the larks, Matt, tell me about these people.'

'I thought they were businessmen. You know what it's been like just trying to keep Prince Simba in the last two years. It gutted me financially. I had to find fifty grand to buy him after he broke down. McCafferty wanted him shot for the insurance.'

'You can't blame him, Matt. The vets wrote the horse off.'

'I knew I could get him back again, Eddie. No fucker believed me. Bet you didn't?'

'I didn't. But you've done it. Mea culpa.'

'I'm not having a go, you know that. It's just been a tough two years.'

'I know. Tell me about the businessmen.'

'Chinese. Rebecca knew them. They looked the part; suited and booted. Their top guy even had a cut-glass accent straight out of Oxford. Lee Sung. Face like a sampan boatman, but all dickied up and talked like a BBC announcer. Anyway, Mister Sung says he and his colleagues want to invest in a racing stable, want to put fifty grand in.'

'For what?'

'Twenty per cent of the business. That valued it at quarter of a mill when the only relation to mill was as in millstone round my neck.'

'They didn't want a share of this?' Eddie patted Prince Simba's neck.

'He was still on the easy list.'

'So when did things go tits up?'

'When I banked their cash. And I mean cash. They brought it in a Tesco bag. The lack of a banker's draft or an alligator skin briefcase should have been my first clue, eh?'

'Gangsters?'

'Chinese gangsters. Triad.'

'Have they asked you to stop horses?'

'That's about the only thing they haven't asked. They want winners. Big priced ones. I offer something at six-to-four and Lee Sung looks at me like I called his mother a whore.'

'You gave them Carpathian yesterday?'

'Lee Sung put twenty five grand on it. He told me this morning they just added the losses to my tab.'

Eddie shook his head. Matt blew his nose. The horses walked the last fifty yards of metalled road leading to the gallops, their shoes clicking a beat way out of rhythm with the birdsong overhead.

'What are you going to do?' Eddie asked.

'Pray.'

'Call the cops in, Matt.'

'No point. I'll tell you how scared of the cops they are, they haven't even mentioned them. Not once. I expected him to warn me before he left this morning not to contact the police. Not a word. Not a fucking jot. That's what they think of the cops.'

'Doesn't stop you calling them in.'

'Pointless. Believe me.'

'So what's the answer?'

Matt shrugged. 'Sit and suffer. Try and do a deal to get them off my back. Find one big fat certainty at fancy odds and offer them double or quits.'

'What if it ends up double?'

'When that fella wins next Saturday, I'll stash away the plane fare to Venezuela and book some in-flight plastic surgery. Grow a beard...rent a cave...hope for the best.'

'Seriously, Matt, come on.'

The trainer pulled his horse up and leant low to open the gate. 'I'm being serious, mate. If you can think of anything better, I'm all ears. Whisper in them while they're still attached to my head.'

They went onto the springy turf. Eddie felt Prince Simba tense up, anticipating the fast work.

'Get going, Eddie. You're sitting on my escape route. Look after him.'

Eddie swung Prince Simba to face the long green incline and the big horse launched himself with a surge that almost fired Eddie into orbit.

As Prince Simba powered along, Eddie smiled through the blurring acceleration until the cold wind made slits of his eyes. This was a proper racehorse. When he finally managed to pull the snorting animal up, Eddie turned him and cantered toward his trainer.

Matt watched them come, the image morphing to a victorious walk into the winner's enclosure at Cheltenham, then Kempton for the King George VI Steeplechase, then maybe, just maybe, Cheltenham again for the Gold Cup.

Before leaving for Taunton, Eddie offered to remove Jinty's remains and help Matt clean up. Matt went out and returned carrying a blue hat box braided with yellow ribbon. 'Not the most appropriate as coffins go, but it's better than an old bin bag. If you'd be kind enough to rest the poor little bugger in it and put him in the cellar, I'll bury him later when none of the lads are around.'

Eddie took the box. 'Do any of them know what happened this morning?'

Matt shook his head. 'I doubt it. I think most were out with the first lot. Lee Sung came in shortly after the string left. Must have been sitting waiting.'

Matt stayed in the kitchen while Eddie gently laid the body in the box. He tried to arrange the head so it didn't look severed, then felt ridiculous for doing so.

Eddie ate a light breakfast. Matt couldn't face food. During the early part of the journey to Taunton, Matt sat quiet, but as Eddie steered them onto the M5 motorway and pushed the Audi up to ninety, Matt said, 'Eddie, will you take over on Prince Simba for the rest of the season?'

Eddie eased off the accelerator. He turned to the trainer. 'In his races, you mean?'

Matt nodded.

'But he's your ride, Matt! You sweated blood to get your licence back for him!'

Matt stared straight ahead. 'My nerve's gone.'

'Bollocks!'

Matt nodded, confirming it quietly to himself. 'My nerve's gone and my concentration's shot. There's no way I can do the horse justice in this state. Will you ride him?'

Eddie glanced across. The ulterior motive didn't take much working out. Should he swallow a big helping of trouble for the chance to ride a top class animal again?

Wiser now than in his championship days, more cautious, his head said *give this a wide berth, Eddie.*

But the wisdom and caution had never reached his heart. 'I'd love to, Matt. Thanks.'

SIX

As Eddie set off on Saturday morning for the short journey south from Shropshire, he switched the radio on, swung right at a junction, flipped the sun visor down against the glare and accelerated toward Cheltenham and the dream of three winners.

Eddie pictured the legions of people making their way to Cheltenham for the Murphy's Gold Cup, the first 'big' race of the season. Among the hordes, none would travel without some thrill of anticipation; gamblers, owners, trainers, jockeys, stable staff. Sixty percent of horses in training never won a race; the sport's lifeblood was that of humanity's - hope and optimism.

Hope, for most of the punters, meant wishing that luck would send at least one winner their way. Two casually dressed middle-aged men on the 9.40 from Paddington to Cheltenham Spa railway station, hoped simply for a photo finish. One, heavily bearded, sat by the window. The leather holdall at his feet contained three very expensive miniature radio communications units and fifty thousand pounds sterling.

Eddie arrived ninety minutes before the first race, threading his way to the weighing room through wandering crowds absorbing the atmosphere, the history, of what many considered the best National Hunt racecourse in the world. Eddie felt a sense of pride riding here.

He was one of the men these people had come to see, although few would have recognized him in suit and tie and gleaming shoes.

Once in a set of racing silks staring out from beneath his skullcap, his face would be familiar to them again.

Eddie always got a buzz just being at Cheltenham; riding a winner there made it special and on that Saturday he rode two. He won the Murphy's Gold Cup on Prince Simba and Matt Nash grabbed him when he dismounted and danced across the winner's enclosure, to the delight of the crowd. The trainer's troubles were forgotten, for a while at least.

But Eddie's next winner brought him most pleasure. He rode a fine tactical race on a wily old hurdler whose challenge had to be delayed to the last second.

As Eddie came coolly to lead a few yards before the winning post, he felt a stab of nervous tension as he glanced across to see that he'd won by a head. He recalled the photo at Newbury and Ken MacAdam's at Stratford, and he resisted riding into the winner's berth until hearing the result of the photo finish.

After weighing in, Eddie pulled a sweater on and went outside to stand on the weighing room steps and reflect on this memorable day.

Eddie stood smiling stupidly. The misery and frustration of the past winnerless weeks evaporated in the warmth of victory. He felt happy, powerful, and supremely confident.

He became aware of someone standing by his shoulder and turned, embarrassed that she might have been there all the time, watching his smug self-congratulation. She was five seven and plump, her bulk covered by a shapeless brown wool coat. The fine hairs of grey fur on her pillbox hat changed patterns as the wind stirred them. Her complexion was smooth, eyes a greyish-blue. Eddie found it hard to guess her age.

'Mister Malloy, my name is Laura Gilpin, I'm a permit trainer. I hope you don't mind me approaching you like this?'

Eddie smiled warmly. 'Of course not. I've seen you around. I'm glad to meet you.'

She let go his hand. 'I thought you gave that horse a brilliant ride. I think it's about the best ride I've seen.'

Eddie's smile widened. She blushed. 'That's not to say I count myself as having great experience, I mean I didn't mean—'

'Talk about a backhanded compliment!'

She squirmed, raising her eyes. Eddie reached to touch her arm. 'I know what you meant, I'm kidding you. Thank you for the kind words.'

She hesitated. 'Would it be terribly cheeky of me to ask you to ride for me at Ascot next Saturday?'

'Which race?'

'The novice hurdle.'

'Fine. I'd be delighted to.'

'Brilliant!'

'You'll be perfect for him,' she said. 'He needs holding up exactly like the chestnut you just won on. Is there any way you could come up and sit on him before Saturday?'

'Remind me again where you train?'

Miss Gilpin looked sheepish. 'Alnwick,' she said quietly.

'*The* Alnwick? Northumberland?'

She nodded, looking suddenly tense.

'Do they still check your passport at the border?'

She smiled again. 'Yes, same place as they issue the oxygen mask and ice axe.'

'Okay. When?'

'Thursday? Sedgefield's on. I thought that maybe if you had a couple of rides there, you could come to me in the morning.'

'I don't know what the northern jocks'll think of a stranger in the camp, but I'll see what I can do.'

'Brilliant!'

Eddie shook her hand. 'See you Thursday,' he said.

'Okay.' She walked away across the parade ring lawn, smiling. Eddie called after her. 'What's the horse's name?'

She turned. 'Samson's Curls.'

Eddie looked puzzled. Miss Gilpin said, 'By Sharpen Up out of Delilah's Dilemma.'

He smiled. 'Nice one, Laura.'

She raised a hand in a small goodbye wave. Eddie said to himself, 'I must be crazy.' He went inside to get ready for the next.

As Eddie's head popped through the neck of the green and gold silks, he found the slight figure of Ken MacAdam beside him. Ken wore his usual wide smile as though he knew something nobody else did. Mid-thirties, with red hair, a big nose and ill-fitting dentures, Ken could talk non-stop. Eddie's heart sank when he saw him.

'How you doing?' Ken asked.

'Okay at the moment. How are you?'

'Put it this way, I didn't ride two winners today, so make your own mind up!'

Eddie smiled and tucked his top into his breeches.

'Any more thoughts on what I told you the other night?' MacAdam asked.

'Not really. Should I?'

'Well something's not right, is it? I got a race I didn't win and so did you.'

'Maybe we should be keeping quiet then, rather than talking about it.'

'You'd be singing a different tune if it was the other way round!'

'I suppose so, but you know what they say, "The camera never lies"'.

'I lost that race at Stratford, Eddie.'

Eddie picked up his helmet. 'Who rode the second?'

'Julian Cross. He agrees with me. He won.'

Buckling his chinstrap, Eddie looked at MacAdam. 'I'm not sure what you want me to do about it, Ken?'

'Well nothing really, I suppose. I just wanted to mention it. What if it happens again?'

'As you said, if I get on the losing end of one, we might see some action.'

'Fair enough.'

Eddie rode a loser in the last and as he came back into the weighing room a blonde woman dashed up and took him by the arm; Rebecca Bow, Matt's new owner. Her eyes shone and the sweet scent he recalled from their first meeting at Newbury meshed now with whiskey fumes. But Eddie thought she looked very alive, very attractive. 'Eddie! Matt asked me to come and find you. He wants you to come up to our box and help us celebrate.'

'I'll be glad to. I'll just get showered and changed.'

Rebecca held onto his arm and walked into the weighing room alongside him, close enough for him to feel her hips swing. She wore a fake fur coat over a figure-hugging charcoal dress. Eddie left her in the main body of the weighing room while he went into the jockeys' room.

Rebecca Bow opened her handbag and took out a small compact mirror. When she flipped it open, a glint of memory from her childhood flashed an image of happier days. Of Sindy dolls, of colouring books, of carefree slumbers. Fleeting. Disturbing, as her adult self confronted her in that disk of harsh light.

SEVEN

Eddie left for Alnwick on a dark and frosty Thursday morning. As he scraped ice from the windscreen of the blue Audi, he wasn't relishing the prospect of riding out on the edge of the North Sea.

Three hours later, with coffee and toast inside him, Laura Gilpin legged him up onto Samson's Curls, a smallish, bay, light framed gelding who looked plain. When she brought the horse out of his box, Laura Gilpin saw disappointment on Eddie's face. 'Don't worry, he's got an engine.'

Eddie thought of a lawnmower engine, convinced he'd had a wasted journey. Laura introduced him to two other riders; girls whose horses were going to help test Samson's Curls. Eddie smiled warmly and said hello.

Stepping onto a concrete mounting block, Laura Gilpin eased herself aboard a big Cleveland Bay and urged him forward. Eddie turned his horse to let her come alongside and all four set off for the gallops.

Laura, at the head of the small string, nudged her mount into a trot as the winding lane led them above the village toward the cliffs.

Once on the turf, the horses wanted to be off. Laura shouted to the riders to wait five minutes until she reached her vantage point.

Not knowing the terrain, Eddie let the girls set the pace. Eddie gave them a ten lengths start and smiled as the easy moving bay cruised up and joined the leaders as they slipped smoothly into top gear. Eddie unleashed Samson's Curls who quickened past his

22

stablemates, just at the point where Laura Gilpin sat grinning on her hack.

Once in front, Eddie felt the little horse lose enthusiasm. Laura had been right, Samson's Curls needed holding up until the last moment.

The trainer sat watching Eddie between the girls, chatting, smiling, and shaking his head. He trotted Samson's Curls up to face her.

'Well?' Laura asked nervously.

'He's good.' Eddie stroked the horse's neck.

'How good?'

'I've won races on a lot worse.'

'Do you think he can win on Saturday?'

'From what I've seen of the rest of them he'll win all right if I don't mess it up.'

'He's a thinker, isn't he?'

Eddie patted the horse's neck. 'Makes Einstein look dumb. Maybe it's immaturity. We'll find out on Saturday.'

Laura stood in the stirrups and did a quick combination of air-punches, then put her hands on her hips and swayed like a belly dancer before settling back in the saddle.

Eddie laughed. 'You do that a lot, don't you?'

'How do you know?'

'Your horse never turned a hair. Most would have wondered if some lunatic had landed on them.'

She patted the big bay. 'He's used to carrying a daft woman around.'

'You look pretty handy with the shadow boxing.'

'I used to be in the circus.'

'You're kidding! I loved the circus when I was a kid.'

'Me too. I *was* kidding. But I'll get there someday. Maybe we could team up? You could catch me on the flying trapeze.'

Eddie eyed her slowly from boot-heels to hat, smiling every wider on the way up. 'I'll pass on that, if you don't mind.'

'Hey! What are you trying to say?'

They laughed together. 'Fancy a paddle?' Laura said. 'Have you got time?'

'Sure. I'm not due at Sedgefield until the second. Bags of time.'

They turned and Laura led them down the winding lane to the empty beach, where the wind-chased sand stuck to the horses' legs.

Gentle breakers rode a turning tide as they went deeper, water washing over the cooling animals at knee height.

Eddie moved his mount alongside the big bay. 'Laura, this is going to sound pretty damn cheeky of me and I feel awkward but…well, are you a gambling stable? I mean, do you plan to have a decent bet on Saturday? I hope you don't mind me asking.'

'As George Washington once said, gambling is the child of avarice, the brother of iniquity and the father of mischief…So we won't be having more than ten grand on him.'

Eddie stared at her, unsure. Amused by his bafflement, Laura laughed showing perfect teeth. 'No, I don't bet, Eddie. I'm in it for days like these. For horses like the one you're sitting on, and the only thing that scares me is that he might be so good I'll become addicted. After seven years of hoping, I'm scared of what he'll do to me.' Laura undid her chinstrap and eased her helmet off, shaking out sandy coloured hair to be blown from behind, matching the pattern of the mane and tail of her mount. 'That's better.'

She looked at the water. 'Soft landing for a hard head.' Her smile widened. 'So I hope that answers your question. I don't know what you've got in mind, but I'm happy for you to make some money on Saturday, if you can.'

'No. That wasn't what I meant. I'm not a betting man either, but there's a friend of mine who's in trouble…he badly needs a result, it would—'

'Fine. Go ahead. I appreciate you asking. A lot of jockeys would have mouthed off without saying anything to me. Help your friend out.'

'You're sure?'

'Absolutely.'

'What about the owner?'

She smiled at him, the wind pushing tendrils of hair across her eyes. 'The owner's happy as well. No problem.'

'You own him, too?'

'Lock, stock and barrel or should that be bloodstock and barrel? Anyway, he's all mine. Tell your friend to fill his boots on Saturday.'

EIGHT

Eddie found Matt Nash in the saddling boxes at Sedgefield, adjusting the girths on an iron-grey mare.

'Hey!'

Matt turned.

'Eddie. What do you know?'

'I got a horse.'

Matt straightened, looking serious. 'Honestly?'

Eddie smiled and moved in to put an arm around the trainer's shoulders in the gloom of the stall. 'Do you think your business partners will go double or quits on a twenty to one shot at Ascot?'

'Where'd you get it from?'

'I ride it. First-timer. Small trainer. Big price.'

'Chance?'

'Great chance. I've won on plenty that are slower, much slower.'

Matt Nash relaxed into Eddie, putting an arm around his waist, almost slumping against him. 'Thank God!'

'It'll be a nervy one, Matt. He pulls up in front. I need to deliver him very late.'

'I don't care how late you deliver him, just as long as you're ahead of everything else when you get there.'

That evening, in a London penthouse apartment, three men sat around a low table drinking coffee and stacking bundles of banknotes like tower blocks, betting on whose would topple first.

The lights of the city through the picture window showed the patterns of streets, too far below to send traffic noise up. A high tech computer system sat on a large black desk in the centre of the room.

Two of the men, Walter and Magnus, had been at Cheltenham the previous Saturday. Middle-aged, they wore their working clothes, mid-range suits and shirts in shades of grey; black leather shoes, loose-laced, years old but travelling companions to these men and capable still of shining.

Coins glinted in upturned cloth caps belonging to Walter and Magnus. The caps rested on the floor, beside a black holdall containing radio equipment.

The third man, thirty-year-old Ben Turco, had suggested the money-stack game, another weapon in his constant battle with boredom. The manic Turco, whose coarse coconut matting hair and round staring eyes gave the impression of a puppet come to life, was creativity on steroids. His maelstrom mind never closed, even in sleep. He spoke, his Boston accent fascinating to Walter and Magnus, who remembered JFK. 'I'm glad we nailed it on the first race on Saturday. Malloy's was the only other close finish and he's one of the good guys.'

'The bookies are suspicious now, Ben. Magnus and I were talking on the trip down. We think it's time to bow out. No offence.'

'None taken, Walter. I believe you're right and anyway, I'm getting bored with it. It's too easy.'

Walter and Magnus glanced at each other. They hoarded smiles, and even such quick agreement from their boss didn't merit anything more than a nod between them.

'But we ought to pull just one more,' Turco said. 'Give 'em pain! Could we get a hundred grand on?'

'We'd do well to get five grand on now, Mister Turco,' said Magnus. 'When were you thinking of?'

'Saturday.'

Walter and Magnus frowned.

'Lighten up, guys. Jeez, I'd swear you were twins sometimes. In ten years, you'll look back and count these as the glory days. Let's do it, then find something else, something more challenging. What do you say?'

'Shall we see what Grimond thinks?' Walter said.

'Grimond's a greedy bastard. I know what he'll say, but I'm happy to give him a call.'

Turco went to the PC screen, put on a headset and clicked his mouse a few times. A ringing tone sounded through the speakers. A man answered. 'Hello?'

'Phil?'

'Ben.'

'Would you be okay for Saturday?'

'Always ready when you are.'

'Good! Magnus will call you tomorrow night with the frequency.'

'I'll be waiting.'

Turco turned to his glum partners, 'Game on, boys! Game on!'

NINE

At Ascot, Laura Gilpin spoke to Eddie as the twelve runners circled in the parade ring. 'Did you pass the information to your friend in need?'

Eddie smiled. 'He was very grateful.'

'He's welcome to join us to watch the race, you know. Is he here?'

'He's busy at home, but I'm sure he'll be watching on TV.'

'Let's hope he'll be watching a winner.'

'Fingers crossed.'

Matt Nash was not at home. If things went wrong, he wanted to be where the Chinese couldn't find him. Rebecca persuaded a friend to allow Matt use of a basement flat in Chelsea that weekend. He sat alone in its opulence, a luxury hideout if things went wrong. What he would do after that he didn't know. He'd lost control of rational thought. His concentration refused to focus on anything except Samson's Curls. If the horse lost, his mind would move to the next vital matter; staying alive. Matt increased the TV volume.

Eddie mounted.

Samson's Curls trotted lightly out of the parade ring and down the horsewalk, spooking as the TV camera came into view, jinking left. Eddie sat tight.

In a dark room in a London nightclub, a cinema-size screen showed Eddie cantering to the start wearing Laura Gilpin's colours of green and gold. A caption listed Samson's Curls' price at 16-1. A

Chinese man speaking on the phone noted down figures. He turned to his colleague. 'All money on. One hundred thirty-five thousand.' His companion nodded and fixed his eyes on Eddie as the tapes went up.

At Ascot, the bookies' betting cries faded as they totted up bets and stuffed cash into satchels. Magnus moved among them, the bearded man from the flat, a tiny speaker in his ear, microphone concealed in his coat collar. Walter leaned on the rails beside the winning post.

At the start Eddie sized up his opponents and thought the favourite, Surrealist, the only horse who might spoil the party.

Matt had no say in his own destiny now.

Eddie settled Samson's Curls in last place. The little horse traveled keenly. Eddie worked to calm him, to kid and cajole, conserve energy for unleashing in the final seconds. Eddie played the bit through the gelding's mouth, trying to take his mind off the competition. The horse relaxed into a regular stride pattern and popped the first four hurdles as he did when schooling at home.

With less than a circuit remaining, Eddie eased past the stragglers, into contention.

They galloped toward the final turn... two to jump before the sprint to the line. Eddie crept stealthily through as the bulk of those under pressure spread out off the bend, and he moved Samson's Curls into fourth approaching the second last hurdle. With daylight in front and his touch paper lit by passing so many horses, Samson's Curls launched himself at the obstacle a stride too soon. But his flair for jumping carried him past the leaders in the air.

'Jeez!' The thrill from the extravagant leap took Eddie by surprise. Then he faced the downside of so much ground gained...hitting the front too soon. Teeth gritted, he rode for the final jump knowing that once it registered with Samson's Curls that there were no more horses to catch, it would be an agonizing run to the line. The hurdle kept the horse occupied until he flew over, then he downed tools.

When a horse stops racing, no amount of force will change his mind. Eddie played him at his own game by shortening the reins and sitting relatively still compared to Surrealist's jockey, who saw he'd been given a second chance.

Murmurs about Eddie's tactics rose in the stands among the punters who were partial or ignorant. Experienced race-readers realized that the huge unexpected leap by Samson's Curls had caught Eddie out; a matter of bad luck rather than poor judgment. But that knowledge did not help Laura Gilpin or Matt Nash feel any better. Separated by twenty five miles and the River Thames, they watched in helpless desperation as Surrealist's nose came upsides Eddie's thigh, then drew ahead with just fifty yards to go.

But Eddie knew that being headed again might rekindle his mount's racing instincts.

It did.

But the winning post loomed as Samson's Curls surged again. Eddie crouched low in a pumping rhythm, his trunk pushing forward as he kicked to encourage his partner to lengthen a little more.

With the red and white disk almost close enough to touch, Eddie let out a scream that echoed in the stands. Samson's Curls lunged forward to escape the noise, and thrust his head in front of Surrealist's a yard from the post.

'Photograph, photograph,' the course announcer's voice rang out.

As they crossed the line, Walter, positioned on the winning post and staring as though trying to look through it, straightened and spoke into the concealed microphone. 'Okay, Phil, let's go. Magnus, Surrealist.'

A few bookmakers chalked up odds on the photo finish: 1/6 Samson's Curls, 9/2 Surrealist. Walter moved calmly among them with sheaves of notes betting Surrealist. The first three or four took his money with a knowing, slightly sympathetic, 'there's one born every minute' look but as he piled on more and more they got nervous and started asking for their tic tac man to confirm his judgment.

Walter continued betting.

Eddie walked the horse toward the winner's enclosure, laughing at Laura Gilpin's air-punching routine as she hurried to meet him. Eddie felt happy too for Matt Nash.

Matt wept. In that beautiful basement flat below the streets of London, he sat in silent tearful relief, as though the weight of twenty storeys of stone above him had been lifted from his bones.

In the cascade of emotions, he thought he was dreaming when the Saturday afternoon BBC sports anchor-man said, 'I'm afraid our team at Ascot called it wrong in that tight finish. The photo shows that the race has gone to Surrealist by the shortest of short heads.'

TEN

Walter moved among sour resentful bookmakers, collecting wads of notes. In the unsaddling enclosure, as her horse was led away, Laura Gilpin stood in stunned silence. Eddie put a hand on her shoulder. 'Laura, I don't know what happened after we passed the post but we passed it first, I don't care what the photo-finish camera says. Let's go and see the print because if it shows Surrealist finishing in front of us I'm going to speak to the stewards.' They set off toward the course noticeboard.

Matt Nash, dazed by the shock, had not yet switched to survival mode. On autopilot, Matt eased his credit card from his wallet. He stared at it for a minute; so many thoughts seeking room in his mind and no way of managing them. He went out and pressed the elevator button. Traveling in the silent silver cube, Matt tried to recall where he'd seen the wine merchant's sign. Just around the corner, in the Kings Road, he believed.

Through the tourists and the traffic noise he moved, zombie-like, amazed that chief among his senses now was smell. His nose sucked in and analyzed the odours of the river; odours, not scents. Not aromas. Not even smells.

Odours.

Malodorous. Good word, Matt thought; appropriate. Malodours: dead fish, dead birds, dead men. Floating corpses. Sunken cadavers.

Mother Thames.

Daddy Death.

He bought champagne. He'd planned to buy champagne and he was damned-well going to have champagne.

'What's the celebration?' The cashier asked

'Life.' It came unbidden, his tongue taking over from his paralyzed mind.

'As good a reason as any!' she said.

Matt nodded.

'Smile!' she said.

The corners of his mouth rose. He didn't blink. Her smile faded. He walked out, swinging the unbagged bottle like a club.

Matt swiped his card and got back into the lobby. He pressed for the elevator. The ground floor indicator lit. A melodic ping announced the elevator's arrival. The silver doors opened. Two Chinese men stood inside and Matt surprised himself by smiling with relief; glad the wait had been short.

ELEVEN

Eddie drove, his Audi heading north, his mind still at the track. He shook his head as he pictured Ken MacAdam telling everyone how he'd warned Eddie. He'd warned him! But he hadn't seemed interested.

Laura had demanded to see the stewards and they'd agreed that although the video 'deceptively showed her horse as the likely winner' the photo-finish print was infallible.

Infallible.

Eddie, finger-combed his hair and sighed then reached to bring up Peter McCarthy's number. McCarthy was a big wheel in Jockey Club Security. As he touched the phone, it rang. Eddie didn't recognize the number.

'Eddie Malloy.'

'Eddie! It's Becky Bow. Matt's in bad trouble!'

Rebecca. A picture of her pretty face came to Eddie's mind.

'What's wrong?' Eddie asked.

'The Chinese got him! They kidnapped him!'

'When?'

'About an hour ago. He was staying at my friend's flat, for safety, you know. I drove over to see him after the race and I saw them push him into a car. I followed them!'

'Okay. Okay. Do you know where Matt is now?'

'He's in a club in Wardour Street in London.'

'Where are you?'

'Outside the club.'

34

'Have you called the police?'

'I called them first. They've been. They went into the club. They said there's nobody in there that's in any trouble at all. They talked to me like I'm some kind of crank. They just wouldn't listen!'

'So where are they now?'

'They've gone. They said they've got enough to do without drunken women making malicious calls.'

'You don't sound drunk.'

'I'm not, for Christ's sake! I had a couple of glasses of bubbly at a party, that's all. Now I don't know what to do!'

'Could they have taken Matt out through a back door or something?'

'I suppose they could. I don't know.'

Eddie looked at the dashboard clock. 'I can be there in half an hour if the traffic's not crazy. Can you stay there?'

'Of course I can! Of course!'

'How big a street is Wardour Street?'

'Don't know. I haven't been to the end of it. Pretty long, I think.'

'I'll call you when I'm closer. You can tell me exactly where you are.'

Rebecca gave him her number. He said, 'If anything changes call me.'

'Okay. I will. Drive safely, Eddie.'

He accelerated. Why phone him? How much had Matt told her in the last week or so and what exactly was their relationship?

Eddie chided himself. He should have thought of Matt earlier, rang him. But Laura Gilpin's distress had taken his mind off Matt and the Triads. Eddie tried to see it from their angle: killing Matt would be pointless; they'd never get their money then.

TWELVE

On a wooden chessboard on a tabletop in the dark basement, Matt Nash's hand leaked blood from a number of cuts. The point of a short sword rose and fell, sticking into the board in the spaces between his fingers. Blood congealed on the nail of his index finger and his hand trembled.

Lee Sung, in his cultured accent, said, 'Remember, Mister Nash, if your hand leaves the board, your hand leaves your body.'

Matt's face glistened in the periphery of the lamplight, red eyes staring downwards in exhausted concentration, sweat darkening the ends of his hair, the ridge of his collar, Adam's apple bobbing as he fought the panic.

'Tell me how you're going to pay back the money?' Lee Sung said. 'One hundred and thirty-five thousand at sixteen to one is well over two million pounds. You owe me two million pounds, Mister Nash.'

Eddie Malloy sweated too, picking and cursing his way through London traffic, drawing ever nearer.

Halfway down Wardour Street, Rebecca Bow's yellow Mercedes sat uneven, partly on the pavement, outside the narrow entrance to the club. Inside the car, Rebecca relaxed, smoked and listened to rock music on the radio, as the human and the metal traffic on Shaftesbury Avenue briefly crossed her eyeline at the narrow canyon end of the dark street.

In the darkened room, Matt Nash was unable to flinch any more as dried blood had stuck his hand to the chessboard. Some of his wounds were an inch long, though most were small deep nicks. In some of these holes, Lee Sung had pushed splinters from the damaged wooden board, arranging the tiny weapons in order of black and yellow paint that still clung to them.

Matt had passed out a couple of times, brought round by frantic slapping of his cheeks. The sweat had dried cold on him and he shivered; moist tear tracks marked his cheeks. He felt he'd been there for days. The muscles in his shoulder and arm burned and ached with the effort of constantly keeping his hand on the board. It had been a long time since he'd looked at the hand itself.

Lee Sung said, 'You won't go home until you tell me how you'll pay me back.'

'I've told you I cannot pay you what you want. I gave you the information on that horse in good faith. I have no way of paying you that kind of money. Maybe I can give you another horse soon and we can hope for better luck. That's all I can keep telling you. That's all.'

The effort of speaking seemed to exhaust Matt and drive him close to tears again. This appeared to please Lee Sung. 'Perhaps your jockey friend, Mister Malloy, can help? He can ride some races the way I tell him.'

'He won't. He's an honest man.'

'There are no honest men.'

Lee Sung brought the sword down taking an aspirin-sized piece of flesh from Matt's index finger and raising it on the tip of the sword to glisten in the lamplight. Matt tensed and grunted and a tear squeezed from his clenched right eyelid. Lee Sung smiled. Two other men watched impassively.

Rebecca Bow took Eddie's call telling her he was minutes away. When Eddie hung up, Rebecca started the Mercedes and drove 300 metres before turning right and parking again half on the pavement. She opened the glove box and took out a handgun. She left the car, dragging her fake fur coat from the passenger seat. She slipped it on and put the gun in a pocket as she walked back toward the club.

THIRTEEN

Eddie's first thought when he saw her under the streetlight, the orange rays catching her blonde hair, was of a prostitute touting for business. Their eyes met and she smiled. She seemed calm. Eddie wasn't. He got out of the car. Rebecca hurried to meet him and offered her cheek for a kiss. Hardly the time for niceties, Eddie thought, but he kissed her lightly then said, 'Is there another way in?'

At the rear of the club, steps led to a concreted basement level. Rebecca followed Eddie down until they reached a double fire door below a window crusted with dirt. Four beer barrels stood under the window. Eddie vaulted onto a barrel and tried to see through the glass.

'Eddie!' Rebecca whispered. The fire-door opened as she pushed it. Eddie jumped down.

With Matt's hand a bloody mess on the chessboard, Lee Sung tried prising it away to make room for his good hand.

The door opened.

Lee Sung turned at the same time as his henchmen to see the pair coming in.

Matt cried out, 'Eddie!' and began sobbing with relief.

Lee Sung smiled. He chopped, neatly taking off Matt's little finger, which Lee Sung picked up and threw at Eddie. Eddie shouted, 'You bastard! ' and lunged toward the Chinaman. His speed and tenacity took Lee Sung by surprise. Lee Sung tried to raise his sword but it had barely cleared shoulder height when

Eddie head butted him, pulping his nose and sending him crashing to the floor. As Eddie followed him down, he bent his legs and parted them to land with one knee grinding deep into Lee Sung's groin and the other smashing into his ribcage.

Lee Sung's men moved quickly to try and take Eddie while he was on the floor. Rebecca stepped forward, pulling the gun and holding it at shoulder height in both hands. 'Back off, fellas! Never heard of a fair fight?'

Fear in their eyes, they retreated. Rebecca said, 'Get on the floor, face first.'

They did and she moved behind them to where she could see Eddie. He had the Chinaman's wrist pinned under his foot, the sword raised in his right hand. Eddie glared at him; Lee Sung's split nose and wrecked mouth hindered breathing. Each exhalation sent bubbles erupting through the mass of blood like geysers on a mudflat. Eddie shouted. 'Which finger would you like to lose, you bastard! Spread them or I'll take your whole fucking hand off! Spread them!'

Lee Sung's fingers, pale from the circulation block caused by Eddie's foot, opened slowly, as if they had a life of their own. Eddie raised the sword, holding it there for what seemed a long time. Rebecca moved, better to see his face, his eyes.

Eddie stepped off the man's wrist and went down on one knee taking a hank of Lee Sung's hair and twisting it until his head came up. 'Look at me,' Eddie said. 'Look at me!' Lee Sung opened his watery, pain-filled eyes. Eddie put the sword point to his neck. 'If you ever come near this man again, or this woman or any other person I know or have known I will take this sword and shove it so far up your arse it'll take your head off from the inside. And that goes for any other crawling Triad rats you might know. Do you hear me?'

Lee Sung grunted. Eddie said, 'And listen…I do not give a toss how many are in your Triad or how big and bad they are. If any of them cause my friends and me trouble of any kind, I'm coming for you. For *you*. Do you understand that?'

Lee Sung grunted again and Eddie turned the sword and swung it toward the Chinaman's head embedding it in the floor by his ear so he could hear the blade vibrate as it settled in the wood.

Eddie stood and seemed to become aware again of the others. He looked at Rebecca. She smiled. His nerves tingled. He couldn't have found a smile the way she had and he admired her cool. Turning, he realized she must have dealt with Lee Sung's henchmen who lay face down at his feet. Puzzled, he glanced again at Rebecca and she held the gun up and winked.

Eddie raised his eyes to heaven. He turned to Matt who seemed transfixed. Eddie said, 'You okay, Matt?' The trainer nodded, looking up at him. Eddie took his good arm and said, 'Can you stand?' Matt clambered to his feet and took a step away from the chair. As his mutilated hand came off the table, the splintered chessboard came with it. Eddie put an arm around him. 'Let's get you to hospital.'

Like a child, Matt rested his head on Eddie's shoulder and, clutching the chessboard to his chest, shuffled forward.

Eddie said, 'Wait a minute,' and started looking around on the floor. Rebecca held out a cotton handkerchief exposing Matt's bloody severed finger. 'Got it,' she said, smiling again.

A surgeon at Bart's Hospital tried unsuccessfully to reattach Matt's finger, but his delicate needlework repaired the rest of his hand. While the surgeon worked, Eddie and Rebecca sat in the waiting room.

Rebecca told Eddie the gun was a replica and she'd been bluffing, that's why she hadn't gone in on her own.

'Well, you're pretty damn cool,' Eddie said.

'And you're pretty damn fiery.'

'Not normally. I lost it completely when that bastard cut Matt's finger off. Jeez, how can you do that in cold blood?'

'You couldn't. I watched you. You thought about it.'

Eddie sighed, rubbing the bristly beard shadow he had now. 'I know. I should've. Just couldn't do it.'

Rebecca nudged him playfully. 'I'm glad.'

'I bet he is too, the bastard.'

Rebecca shifted in her seat as she felt herself growing moister, warmer low in her belly. She'd never experienced such a surge of libido.

She said, 'Were you afraid?'

Eddie hesitated. 'I don't know. Didn't really have time to think about it.'

'How do you feel now?'

Eddie shrugged. 'Still angry. Sorry for Matt. Guilty that I forgot about him after the race.'

They settled Matt in Eddie's car. Eddie turned to Rebecca. 'Are you coming with us? I'll stay the night at Matt's place.'

She smiled in the darkness as the cold wind caught her hair, blowing wisps across her face. 'I've got to get home, I'm afraid.'

'Where's that?'

'Normally, St John's Wood but my flat's being decorated so I'm at the Dorchester at the moment.'

'Nice place.'

She pushed tendrils of hair away from her mouth. 'It's okay.'

Eddie hesitated. 'Can I call you?'

'I'll come looking for you if you don't.'

FOURTEEN

Eddie set out for Newmarket. He planned to stay overnight there with his mother and his sister. From their small stud farm, it wasn't far to Huntingdon where Eddie was riding next day, if the track thawed in time.

The further east Eddie travelled, the more convinced he became that there'd be no racing in Britain for a few days, let alone at Huntingdon in less than twenty-four hours. The countryside was white. Snow and ice narrowed many of the B roads to single tracks.

About thirty miles west of Newmarket, Eddie took a call from Peter McCarthy of Jockey Club security. 'Mac. Where are you holed up? Somewhere warm, no doubt?'

'Warm, dry and close to a coffee machine.'

'Stay there. It's tough out here in the real world. What can I do for you?'

'Tell me what's happening with these photo-finishes.'

'I wish I knew. You seen mine?'

'Twenty times. And Ken MacAdam's, and Bobby Tobin at Newbury where you got the result.'

'What's your thoughts?'

'Officially? We're getting ready to organize expert checks on the photo equipment at every single track. Unofficially, we're baffled. We've had someone quietly look at the three cameras involved, and all the supplementary stuff. Not a sign of malfunction anywhere.'

'Somebody is tampering with the prints, aren't they?'

'It's too early to say, Eddie, I'm waiting for copies of the prints themselves.'

'Do yourself a favour, Mac, don't get copies get the originals.'

'What's the difference?'

'Well, something's going on with these photos. You'd better keep your suspicions to yourself, for now. If you start asking the technical guys for copies, you might alert whoever's behind it. Why don't you just quietly call the racecourse managers for the original prints?'

'I'm not certain they always keep them.'

'It's worth a phone call to find out.'

'Okay, leave it with me.'

The weather worsened. More than five hours after setting off, he finally reached the Malloy stud. Driving under the entrance arch dulled his mood and he wondered if that would ever change.

Marie, his sister, greeted him as he walked to the door and he thought how much she resembled their mother as Eddie remembered her from childhood: dark shoulder length hair, bright blue eyes, wide mouth, slightly upturned nose peppered with faint freckles, which Eddie knew, would spread and darken come summer. The family had been apart for fourteen years and Eddie had not yet grown used to seeing his sister as a woman - she'd been thirteen when he'd left home.

Approaching her, he returned her smile and they hugged. 'I thought you'd got lost'

'Roads are bad. Passed quite a few abandoned cars.'

She ushered him in with a hand on his arm. In the kitchen, they waited for the kettle to boil. 'Mother still in bed?'

'She seems to live there now.'

'I'll go up and say hello.'

'She's asleep. Wakes at night, sleeps all day. At midnight, she switches on that old cassette deck. Remember it?'

'Too well.'

'Same tape, same bloody dirges, over and over.'

'Ask her to stop or to keep it low.'

'She plays it low, but that seems to make it worse. It drifts through the house like air. Like vapour. I lie awake and sometimes think I can see the notes, the treble clefs, the minims, the crotchets like you used to see on the old cartoons. They settle over my bed in the dark.'

Eddie sat down again. 'She's not in father's old room, is she?'

'She's in the big room at the front. She's been talking about moving into dad's old room.'

Eddie hated the dull dingy room his father had insisted on spending the final months of his life in, the room in which he'd hidden away from Eddie.

He looked at Marie. 'So I guess it doesn't quite feel like home to you yet?'

Marie shrugged, 'I don't know that I ever thought it would.'

'Regrets?'

'When I sold up to move in here, I was hoping mother would keep improving. That plan for companionship is turning into nursing.'

'I think it's just a phase, Marie, a relapse. Winter could have brought it on. He'll be a year dead next month.'

'I know. I hope it's not the winter. It's a long time until spring.'

'She'll pick, up, I'm sure.'

Marie nodded slowly, looking at him, both knowing what fuelled the look. It had been Eddie's idea that Marie sell her own house and buy half the stud, move in with mother. That was his way out. He wasn't sure if Marie had realized that at the time. Looking at her, he knew she did now. A change of subject was needed.

'Sit down,' he said, 'I'll make the tea.' He picked up the kettle and spoke over his shoulder, 'Did you ever meet Granville Bow, the guy who owned the big mail order empire?'

'I've heard of him. Never met him. I thought I read he was dead?'

'He is. Owned a lot of decent horses at one time. I used to ride for him. I'm taking his daughter out to dinner soon.' He put a blue tea mug in front of her on the table.

'After her fortune, are you?' Her smile held little warmth.

'Yep, gold-digging's my business.'

'What's she like?'

'Lovely. Natural blonde, very-'

'How do you know she's a natural blonde? Or shouldn't I be asking that?'

'Eyebrows. First thing I noticed.'

'Eyebrows can be dyed too, you know.'

'Rebecca's aren't. Trust me.'

She smiled again. 'So, she's blonde, natural blonde, and she's how old?'

'Hmm, about twenty three, I'd say.'

'Likes mature men, does she?'

'She's sophisticated and funny. And ballsy, very ballsy.'

'Too much information, brother!'

Eddie had planned to tell Marie about how Rebecca had helped rescue Matt, but he realized now he didn't know his sister much better than he knew Rebecca. Was Marie gently teasing or trying to make a fool of him? He reached for his coffee and stood, 'I think I'll creep up quietly and just look in on mother.'

'Don't wake her. Unless you want to sit with her all night.'

'Even if I wanted to sit with her all night, ten minutes is about all she can stand me for.'

'So why don't you just bail out once and for all, Eddie? You're playing at this, this brother and son business.'

Her back was to him. She didn't turn. He moved to where he could see her face and waited for an apology, but her look stayed hard. 'I'd pick easier games to play, Marie. Ones I might enjoy. You stood at the graveside with me last Christmas, remember? Hand in hand, all three of us. New start? That means we were all supposed to try.'

'That's exactly what it meant, Eddie. Now you're a hundred and fifty miles away.' Marie looked at the ceiling, 'She might as well be a hundred and fifty miles away. From where I sit, there's only one person who kept that deal we made at the graveside.'

Eddie sat down again and looked at her across the table. 'What do you want me to do? Move in with you? Or do you want out?'

'All I do is run up and down those bloody stairs a hundred times a day. For what? Even I don't know why I'm doing it. Can you tell me?'

The tough edge had gone from her, or maybe Eddie could see past it now to the despair. He softened. 'Tell me what you want, Marie. I'll do whatever I can.'

She clasped her hands and leaned across at him, chin low, eyes drilling up into his face. 'Do you know what I want? I want her to have what she wants. Death.'

FIFTEEN

Two hundred and fifty miles north-west of Newmarket, among the hills of the northern Lake District, the snow was much deeper. At times, it touched the belly of the strong fell pony, which carried Kim Oliver in the search for his father. Kim had not seen him since the previous day when the farmer set out to rescue their sheep. The boy stayed at home to study, as roads to his school were impassable.

Kim sat up through the night waiting for him, nodding off from time to time in front of the fire he kept banked up to warm his father on his return. But come dawn Kim was still alone, and worried now. His father was an experienced hill farmer and he'd known him to spend a night out in the past when conditions were bad, but this time something gnawed at Kim's gut. He picked up the telephone to call the police; no dial tone. Kim decided to saddle Crystal, his pony, and start searching.

Kim was twelve and Crystal two years older, and the pony knew these hills better than her rider did. They headed westward toward the ranks of snow-topped fells around Kirkstone Pass. Crystal's were the only visible tracks in the white desert of humps and hollows and waist-high padded ridges that were dry-stone walls. Yesterday's terrifying winds had sculpted these strange soft shapes, and moved on, leaving a silent morning. Only the crunch of Crystal's hooves could be heard and a worried but hopeful Kim imagined the sound carrying to where his father would hear it and know he was coming to find him.

It seemed to the boy that he and Crystal had wandered for miles. Despite his warm jumpers and fleece and his long wax coat, the extra socks and thick leather boots, the cold drilled his bones, draining optimism and hope. He realized if he were this cold when constantly on the move and with the heat from Crystal's body to sustain him, that his father would be freezing by now unless he'd found shelter. But Kim urged Crystal on to check one more gully. He looked anxiously at the pale sun and it seemed to him as weary as he was; weary of winter, of cold and of short days.

Crystal's step hadn't faltered even though she'd never been less than hock deep in snow. Icy stalactites hung from her belly but she kept her head down and pushed forward, often ploughing a trail with her barrel chest when she couldn't get her feet high enough. Kim spoke to her frequently, encouraging her, sharing his troubles, wondering aloud where his father was and asking the pony if she thought they'd find him soon.

Crystal had become everything to him. Although he loved his father, all physical affection died with his mother two years ago. The cancer that killed her lived on in him in the form of a pining empty hole forever seeking a seal; something that fitted tight enough to stop the tiniest leaks of sadness.

Kim's classmates lived too far away for him to have proper friendships. Adults too were strangers to Kim. Apart from his teacher, his parents were the only grown-ups he'd really known. He'd never met an aunt or uncle or heard one mentioned. Animals were his companions.

He rubbed Crystal's right ear with his gloved hand. 'Come on, Crys, we'll check Buckbarrow Gully then head for home, I promise.' The little black pony flicked her left ear back as though acknowledging and agreeing the deal, and Kim steered her north to the ridge where the land fell away toward Buckbarrow Crag. At the foot of the crag, in a shallow cave, Kim found the frozen corpse of his father.

SIXTEEN

On Thursday, racing resumed at Uttoxeter and Eddie Malloy went there for two rides. Also at Uttoxeter were Ken MacAdam and Bobby Tobin, who'd suffered the same fate at Newbury as Eddie at Ascot. All three sat on the slatted bench in the corner of the weighing room sipping black coffee, saddles resting on metal racks above them, and racing colours sharing hanging space with their daily clothes on hooks around the walls. Portable calor gas heaters warmed the place, cooking up stale smells of sweat and damp, old socks and tobacco smoke, saddle soap and boot polish.

Ken MacAdam's big-nosed face looked intense. 'Couldn't figure it for days until I spoke to Bobby. Remember I told you Julian Cross rode that horse I'm supposed to have beat in the photo? He told me he got a Jiffy bag through the door a couple of days later. Cash. No note, no questions asked. Two thousand four hundred and sixty-five pounds. Thank you and goodnight.'

'Same with me,' said Bobby Tobin, 'exact amount I'd have won at Newbury.'

'And did the trainer get his percentage?' Eddie said.

'To the penny.' said MacAdam.

'All cash? No letter?'

'Nothing. Money. Right there. In a Jiffy. End of story.'

Tobin drew on a thin roll-up cigarette and crossed his legs.

'No postmarks?'

Tobin and MacAdam shook their heads. Tobin said, 'Hand delivered. Late at night or very early in the morning.'

'Weird,' Eddie said.

'Expect yours any day,' MacAdam told him.

Eddie said, 'I'd better call Laura Gilpin. She was the trainer and owner. Wonder if she'll get all hers in one package?'

'I wonder who's sending them?' said Tobin.

MacAdam said, 'Probably some crank who's seen the photos and feels sorry for us.'

Eddie smiled. 'Some crank!'

'Rich crank!' Tobin said.

Eddie pondered. 'How about it being the guy who's fiddling the photos. Doesn't mind skinning the bookies but gets a guilty conscience over the dupes?'

'In that case,' said Tobin, 'how does he get to pay the thousands of innocent punters who've done their money?'

'And more to the point,' said MacAdam, 'how's he fiddling the photos?'

'And what are Jockey Club Security planning to do about it?' said Tobin.

Eddie went outside to ring McCarthy then Laura Gilpin.

SEVENTEEN

In Ben Turco's London penthouse, the farewell party he'd planned was short one guest. Turco, Magnus and Walter who'd worked closely together throughout the project had been at the flat more than an hour waiting for Phil Grimond, the man who'd been central to the operation. They'd passed the time playing a new game invented by Turco on his PC.

Phil Grimond arrived at eight o'clock. Turco registered his entrance from the corner of his eye and called a warm welcome asking him to make himself comfortable for a minute, 'while I finish off Captain Fantastic and the Brown Dirt Cowboy here!'

'Make it fast,' Grimond said. 'I've got better things to do than piss around here.'

Turco finished his game while Grimond fixed a drink at the bar and settled himself on the couch. Grimond was around five nine, four stone overweight, early thirties, but balding significantly. He had a thick black moustache and a heavy beard shadow. The blue shirt under a tan suit was missing the top button. A sheen of sweat glinted on his forehead; six of his fingers bore gold rings. The chunky bracelet on his right wrist clinked against his watch as he raised the glass.

Turco hurried across to shake hands and welcome him properly. 'How you doin', Phil?'

'Fine.' Grimond drank. 'Couldn't you have sent one of them with the dough like you normally do? Why drag me down here?'

'For a final team drink.' Turco smiled, showing expensive teeth. He turned to the others. 'Come on, guys, bring the bubbly and the glasses!'

Walter and Magnus approached side by side, carrying ice bucket and a silver tray. They nodded to Grimond. He acknowledged them with a dismissive look and stared at Turco. 'Did you say final?'

'That's right,' Turco said. 'End of the old trail ride. Saturday marked the last round-up.' He pulled the magnum dripping from the bucket and filled four glasses.

'Says who?'

Turco offered the glass. Grimond didn't even look at it.

'Listen Phil, we think we've gone as far as we can go with this. The bookies are getting wise. Aren't they, boys?'

Magnus nodded his big head, looking serious. 'They're onto us now, it's too risky to carry on.'

'And what risks have you been taking? I've been the one taking the risks. I'm at the sharp end.'

'And you've been paid well,' Turco said. 'And now we're all getting out before we get caught. We've taken the best part of £350,000 off the bookies inside a month and it's time to say thank you and goodnight, applaud the fat lady, lock up the theatre and find a new show somewhere else. The word on the course is that the jockeys are getting suspicious. These guys know when they've won a race, doesn't matter what the photo finish tells them. It's time to get out, Phil.'

Grimond said, 'We can do at least two more.' It sounded like an order.

'No, we can't,' Walter said.

Grimond sat forward menacingly. 'Who rattled your cage?'

Magnus said, 'Listen, Phil, we're not doing any more.'

'You listen to me. We're doing two more!'

Turco said, 'You might be doing two more but not with us. You'll get your money now and we're finished.' Turco got up and fetched the leather holdall.

Grimond said, 'Listen, Turco, you do two more with me or I tell the police everything.'

Turco kept walking away from him speaking as he moved. 'And land yourself in the shit too?'

'I'll turn Queen's Evidence, probably get probation. You're looking at five years each.'

Turco stopped and turned; he looked at Grimond then at the others. 'You're serious, aren't you?'

'You better believe it.'

Turco got the holdall and came back, undoing the straps as he walked. He knelt on the rug by the couch and emptied out banded wads of notes. He said, 'Let's split this then talk.'

Walter left London later that evening with three Jiffy envelopes filled with banknotes, and two addresses. The thought of the journey to Shropshire didn't faze him but the prospect of reaching Northumberland before dawn made him shiver and he wished it had been Magnus's turn for the delivery. He'd promised himself and Hannah, his wife, a month in Spain and she was already packed. Now he'd have to roll home next morning and tell her Grimond had messed up their plans. Pulling off the M25 onto the M40 Walter said to no one in particular, 'For every decent bloke you meet there's an arsehole waiting round the corner.'

EIGHTEEN

On the way home from Uttoxeter Eddie had a call from McCarthy, the Jockey Club Security officer. McCarthy said, 'The photo-finish operator on each occasion was a man called Phil Grimond. He's worked on the technical side for five years. Not the most likeable human being in the world apparently, but he has a clean history apart from his personal life.'

'Meaning?'

'Got a taste for young boys.'

'Paedophile?'

'Not as far as I know but I'm told he uses rent boys.'

'So if he's involved in some scam a third party could be blackmailing him.'

'Everything's possible. Anyway, he could stand an interview. I plan to go and see him tomorrow.'

'Is that wise, Mac? Even if Grimond is involved, he might not be behind the whole thing. Whoever's running it must be pretty smart.'

'Well he'd have to be ultra-smart because I've been reminded that as from around six months ago, we don't even use photo prints any more. Everything's done from the video. There's no developing involved. The horses are freeze framed on video as they cross the line and a printout of the screen image produced within about a minute. And the operator sits right there in the same box as the judge.'

Eddie whistled through his teeth. 'How the hell are they doing it, then?'

McCarthy said, 'That's why I think we need to speak to Grimond sooner rather than later.'

'Mac, do me a favour and give me a couple of days on this before you do anything. I've a feeling I might be able to pin something down.'

'Eddie, we can't risk it happening again.'

'Listen, it's pointless confronting Grimond when you haven't any evidence. A simple denial from him and it leaves you nowhere, gives him a get-out and if someone else is running it he simply finds another stooge to replace Grimond.'

'Maybe, but what's your solution?'

'Give me forty-eight hours.'

McCarthy sighed. 'Someday, you and me are going to sit down with a calculator and add up all the forty-eight hours and the twenty-four hours and the couple of days you've asked me for in the past three years.'

'Well don't forget to draw up another column to count the pints of blood and sweat I traded off for them.'

'Drama queen.'

Walter reached Eddie's place just before midnight. He'd learned that the more dedicated jockeys would be in bed by ten or half past, ready for an early rise, either to ride out or make a long trip to the races. He'd discovered that Eddie lived in the top-floor flat at this yard.

He parked the car in the trees half a mile away and walked stealthily down the track.

In his coat pocket were a dozen dog biscuits, which he'd found would keep farm dogs quiet enough, most times, to let him get in and out. The worst of the snow had gone and he made little noise as he walked. The pallid moon was more than half-full. He saw the dark hulk of the barn conversion against the sky as he approached.

He pulled the Jiffy from his pocket.

Just a small bag.

As he passed the rear of the building, someone stepped from the shadows and placed a cold metal tube below his left ear. The shock made Walter draw such a huge breath he choked and doubled over into a heavy coughing fit.

NINETEEN

It had been a week since he'd found his father dead and the images of that day and night haunted Kim. Pictures of him as he lay huddled in bright mountain clothing, dusted with ice crystals, bound to the ground by the ice-melt that had leached all the heat from him...the hardness of his flesh...Kim imagined he could have rapped his knuckles on his father's cheeks and heard the echo up the valley. The long trek then through the gathering dusk looking for a farm with a telephone...the sound of the RAF helicopter coming over the fields, its search beam raking Buckbarrow Gully then picking out that sparkling body so starkly as though spotlighting the final act in the darkest of theatres.

Kim tried to push the rest from his mind. The post-mortem revealed a broken back and broken leg. A sheep was found trapped in a small crevasse in the gully. The police concluded that Arthur Oliver had been trying to reach the sheep from the gully edge and had fallen and frozen to death as he lay injured. The sheep survived.

Social Services came for Kim next day and brought him to a grim children's home on the outskirts of Carlisle. This square concrete prison. This small room. This strange smelling single bed against the grimy wall. Apart from the numbing grief, he worried about Crystal and the dogs and two cats. And the sheep, the lifeblood of the hill farm, the reason the farm existed.

Mr Young of Social Services assured him 'provision would be made'. Mr Young, who'd seemed very annoyed when Kim insisted on knowing exactly what he intended doing about the animals.

Mr Young finally admitted that the stock had been dispersed among Kim's three 'neighbours' (the closest farm was seven miles away), who'd agreed to 'collectively assume the burden until more permanent arrangements can be made'. Kim heard some of the adults in the home discussing the fact that no relatives of the Olivers could be traced.

As each day dragged past, Kim felt increasingly isolated and terribly homesick. Though he knew there would be nobody at the farm, not even Crystal (who'd been taken in temporarily, Mr Young said, by Mr Durkan at Clent Fell).

He longed for something familiar, like the smell, the warmth of his pony. Tears flowed as he lay in the darkness, but he dried them, made himself sit up, propped on his elbow feeling the tug of these strange pyjamas.

Kim decided he wouldn't spend another night in this place. He'd run away, return to the farm. He could fend for himself there, hide from Social Services when they came searching. He knew the hills like he knew his own bedroom, he and Crystal did. He'd walk to Mr Durkan's tomorrow night and get Crystal, slip away with her in the darkness. Excited now, and determined, he pushed the covers back and swung his legs out of bed. He'd take the pillow slips with him to wrap around Crystal's hooves so Mr Durkan wouldn't hear them leaving.

No. Bad idea.

That would be stealing, and he didn't want to give them any more reason to come after him. Besides, he needed nothing from this place; wanted nothing, no memory of it. Come dark tomorrow evening he was going.

TWENTY

Inside Eddie's flat a subdued Walter sat facing the jockey, who was feeling pleased with himself. After his conversation with the others at Uttoxeter, he'd decided to stake his own place out, knowing he'd stand a good chance of nailing the delivery man. That was why he'd asked McCarthy to be patient.

Eddie could see why they'd chosen Walter…your everyday man in the street: difficult to guess his age, medium height and build, mousey hair, no striking features, seemingly bland personality - just the type. Potential victims of the scam, like bookmakers, would be hard pressed to compile a photo-fit of this man. He sat subdued, in his grey raincoat, cloth cap on his lap.

Eddie expected him to be angry when he discovered he'd been captured by someone armed with nothing more than a narrow piece of copper pipe, but Walter seemed simply resigned to his fate.

Eddie brewed tea. Walter thanked him politely and sipped from the yellow mug. Eddie said, 'Do you have an envelope for Laura Gilpin?'

Walter nodded.

'Were you supposed to deliver it tonight?'

Another nod. Another sip of tea.

'Long way to Alnwick.'

'I drew the short straw.'

Eddie smiled. 'Tough break.'

'I was supposed to be going to Spain with the missus.' Doleful now.

Eddie liked this man. The least likely criminal he'd ever seen. He resisted a smile of amusement lest he offended Walter. 'Be nice this time of year, Spain,' Eddie said.

Walter perked up. 'We go every year. We're planning to retire there if we can get enough money.'

'I'd've thought this little scam would have set you up with the price of a medium sized villa?'

'Well, we wanted one with a bigger pool.'

Eddie watched him closely, certain that he must be taking the piss. But Walter seemed serious, almost as though chatting to a neighbour over the garden fence. 'That's a shame,' Eddie said.

Walter nodded. 'Yes.' And sipped tea again, adjusting his cap on his lap.

'Did Grimond get the same share as you and the others?'

'We all got…' He stopped and looked at Eddie. 'How did you find out about Grimond?'

'Oh, Jockey Club Security has been onto him for a while. I think they plan to pick him up tomorrow.'

Knees together, cradling his tea, Walter began to rock gently in the chair and stare at the carpet. He said, 'What's going to happen to me?'

'That depends. Will you tell me who's behind the whole thing?'

Walter shook his head. 'That wouldn't be fair.'

'No more than it would be fair for you and Grimond to take the full flak on this. It's a major fraud. You could be looking at five to seven years.'

'And what difference will it make if I tell you who organised it all?'

'Maybe none. But you never know. We might be able to reach some agreement.'

'I respect the fact that you're not promising me anything falsely, Mister Malloy.'

Eddie had to resist a smile again.

Walter said, 'Would you mind if I used your phone?'

'Feel free.'

'Will you promise not to note the number I dial?'

'Promise.' Eddie was beginning to think he'd been trapped in some weird children's game. He watched Walter put his tea down carefully and walk to the phone at the window. With his back to Eddie, he dialled. 'Hello, it's Walter. I'm afraid I'm in a little bit of trouble.'

Eddie listened to him explain. Walter made quiet apologies, but no excuses, telling it exactly as it happened. After a couple of minutes, he hung up and turned to Eddie. 'I think you can expect a call in a short while,' Walter said, then returned to his seat and his tea.

Eddie asked no further questions. They stared at the telephone. Three minutes later, it rang.

'Eddie?'

'That's right.'

'You're a wily old fox.' American accent, amusement in the voice. 'I should have told them not to pull one with you.'

Eddie believed he should know that voice and so did the owner of it who kept talking. 'A victimless crime, Eddie. Bear that in mind. Only the bookies suffered.'

'What about the punters?'

'As many won as lost. As always.'

'That's not the way to look at it.'

'Lighten up, Ed, you were never this serious when we rode together.'

'Ben Turco.'

'Eddie Malloy. I wondered how long it would take you.'

'I think we'd better meet, Ben.'

'I think you're right, Ed. Come to London tomorrow, and I'll buy you dinner.'

'No, thanks. Last time I was there, a little yellow guy tried to trim a few pounds off me, which I'd sooner have lost in the sauna. You come here.'

'Aw shit, Eddie! When? I'm busy!'

'Too bad. You'd better come and bail your pal out.'

'Now?'

'No. I need some sleep. Make it tomorrow night. Buy me dinner here.'

'You're in the middle of nowhere, man! Do they know how to cook up there? Has fire been invented?'

'I'll tell them to start rubbing the sticks together.'

When he'd hung up, Eddie let a surprised and relieved Walter go home, then made coffee and sat by the window marvelling over

Turco's change of career. He'd last seen the American three years ago when Turco retired after eighteen months as an amateur jockey. He'd been a talented rider but lacked nerve. They'd had a few drinks together. Eddie always found him entertaining.

How the hell had the Yank got involved in this? The guy was rich. His father, a Boston industrialist, was a billionaire who'd financed his son's riding career until Ben chucked racing at the age of twenty-five, to 'make his own fortune'. Well he'd certainly tried to do that.

Eddie smiled as he reflected. If the police were to be involved, he would find it tough to hand Turco over.

But then again, nice guy Turco had caused Matt Nash one hell of a lot of grief, and cost him a finger and a few hours of torture. Eddie phoned Matt every day; he was still a frightened man.

And Rebecca? Sexy Becky Bow. He wondered how she was. He'd rung her at the Dorchester a few times but she'd been out. Not wanting to appear desperate, he hadn't left any message.

Rebecca had his number. Why hadn't she called? He decided that if he didn't hear from her over the weekend, he'd give her another call. Ask her out. You never knew where it might lead.

TWENTY-ONE

Turco turned up at Eddie's flat on Saturday evening, still complaining about having to leave London and come out 'to the sticks'. He followed Eddie upstairs making shivering noises as he hurried toward the gas fire. He stood with his back to it, staring through round, steamed-up specs. He wore a long dark green overcoat and a khaki scarf. Although it had been three years plus since he'd seen him, Eddie saw the Yank hadn't changed; the intense pinpoint eyes, the rough coconut hair that Eddie recalled making rasping noises when Turco used to pull on his crash skull.

Reaching under his buttoned coat, Turco dug into the waistband of his trousers and pulled out a section of denim shirt to wipe his glasses on.

'Can't you afford a hankie?' Eddie asked.

Without looking up Turco said, 'I can afford a whole damn cotton plantation, but I like to wipe my glasses on my shirt.'

'I won't ask where you wipe your nose,' Eddie said, sitting down in the easy chair.

Turco put his glasses on and, smiling, drew his coat sleeve across under his nose then said, 'You look pretty fresh for somebody who had four rides today.'

Eddie had ridden at Warwick, less than half an hour's drive away, and had been home in time to shower and change into clean blue jeans and a maroon sweatshirt. Beside him on the small table by the fire sat a glass of whiskey and ice. He sipped it and watched Turco, marvelling at the guy's attitude. You'd think he'd been

61

caught after a game of hide and seek rather than a major scam. He waited until Turco took off his coat then poured him a whiskey and soda.

Turco finished the drink in three swallows, asked for a beer, then settled into the corner of the soft dark blue couch, eased off his loafers and lifted his right leg until he lay half stretched out.

Eddie said, 'Well?'

'You wanna hear the full story?'

Eddie knew how the guy could talk. 'I'll settle for the highlights.'

Turco smiled, settled deeper, swigged some beer and started talking. 'When I came over here four years ago to ride in England for a season, it wasn't for the sport. I'd developed a system for betting horses over jumps. Now racing over jumps back home takes place about as often as an orgy in a convent, as you probably know, and I needed to play regularly. The beauty of betting on jump racing here is that you can learn all about the horses. The same ones appear season after season giving you the chance to learn their characters, which courses they favour, what ground suits them and, well, I don't have to tell you.

'Anyway, I had developed this computer system for analysing everything about a horse, not only its track form but everything from its breeding to whether the lad who looked after it loved it gave it a goodnight kiss. I knew the system would work and that it would make me heaps of money and that it would help me show my dad that you didn't have to be in industry or big business to make a million.

'The one thing I wasn't sure of was that jump racing in England was straight. You know the stories, you've heard them yourself. You understand what I'm saying, Eddie?'

Eddie nodded and watched him, studied this intense little dynamo who gulped his beer and sat up, sliding forward to sit on the edge of the couch as he warmed to this.

'Now, I could have paid for information, mixed it with the bookies and the tough guys, the hard-bitten regulars at the races every day, schmoozed with the touts and the sharpies at night, but I didn't. Know why? Because I had to get the knowledge from the inside. I had to learn by doing it, by taking part, by mixing with you guys in the weighing rooms up and down the country, by going out there and riding round with you, against you, competing, watching, listening, finding out exactly how it was, how straight it was, who the bullies were, who the men with the influence were and seeing how they used it.

'And I don't have to tell you what I found, Eddie. The game was about as straight as a man could pray for. Straighter! Ninety-five per cent straight when the best I'd thought I'd find it would have been seventy-five and even at that I'd have made plenty, let me tell you. So when I calculated ninety-five per cent reliability, you can imagine the hurry I was in to hang up my boots.'

He drank more beer, the gas from it seeming to pop his eyes even wider. He put the can on the carpet and as he sat up again he burped loudly. 'Pardon me! Listen, I believed you guys were crazy. I used to drive to Plumpton and Kelso and Southwell and all those other godforsaken places for just one ride, knowing lots of you were doing the same. I'd watch you go out on a bad novice in the cold and the rain and the mud with nothing in your stomachs but black coffee and butterflies, and I'd sit there waiting to see who'd come back in the ambulance.

'And I'll tell you something, Eddie, I never was so glad to be born into money!' He raised an explanatory hand. 'Don't get me wrong! I'm not being boastful or trying to bring up a class thing, God knows there's enough of that over here already. What I'm saying is, I felt genuine relief and not a little humility that I was doing it through choice.'

'We all do it through choice,' Eddie said, leaning forward to lower the heat on the fire.

'Okay, accepted. But you get what I mean. I could quit when I wanted. Most of you guys can't. Most of you are addicted. You don't know anything else.' Turco opened both hands as though his point was obvious. 'It's a slow form of Russian roulette, Eddie, several games each day, a spin of the barrel every time you swing up into that saddle. And you can't duck out. You won't stop until you find one in the chamber, then it'll be too late.'

'Maybe.' His preaching was beginning to irritate Eddie. 'Go on. We haven't got all night.'

'Okay, fine. Sorry, Eddie. I'm trying to get across how important it all was to me.'

'You're doing just that. Cut to the chase.'

'Okay, long story short. I knew you guys were trustworthy. I quit riding, took a flat in London, set up my system and started milking bookmakers for a living. Within eighteen months, I'd won two and a half million dollars. By then, I couldn't get on any more. Every bookie closed my account. I moved the operation on course for a while but they limited my stakes so much it wasn't worth continuing. I tried a few agents around the country, and wrung another six months and half a million out of that before the bookies got wise and blanked the agents.

'It was becoming like an everyday nine to five job again and I thought, the hell with it! I'll figure out another way to nail them.' He raised the beer can again, pressing it so hard to his mouth it left a pink teardrop shape on his top lip. Turco shuffled his feet and rearranged his thin body into a comfortable position for the next burst.

Elbows on knees, and hands clasped he went on. 'I messed around with a few things which didn't really work out when, just as I was considering quitting, the authorities go and introduce something that they might as well have delivered to me first in a gift box the size of the Ritz.' His curiously round brown eyes sparkled and Eddie noticed in them the reflection of the gas fire's burning columns.

Turco smiled widely, wildly. 'They brought in the still photo finish picture. On screen. Immediate. No print. No developing. Just a frozen image from video as the horses passed the post. Know what I said to that, Eddie? Wanna know what I said? Apart from thank you very much my lords I said, dim. I said, dim, Eddie, D-I-M. An acronym, which belies the name; misleads the innocent listener. For dim read smart, read very smart! ' Eddie waited, wondering if Turco's ancestors had ever run those travelling medicine shows in the Old West.

'Dim stands for Digital Image Manipulator. It was an idea I'd been messing round with for a while based on the sophisticated technology in movie making. It's all technical so I won't bore you.'

Eddie raised his eyebrows. Turco lifted a finger and laughed. 'Got me! Listen, what it means in essence is that the operator of the photo-finish freeze frame can, with DIM software installed, change the finishing positions on screen almost instantly so that the judge, by the time he's watched the others pass the post live, as it were, and turned to the screen to check the photo, sees exactly what we want him to see. He has no choice but to call the result as he sees it on screen.'

Eddie said, 'By which time you've made a killing among the bookies betting on the outcome of the photo finish.'

'Correct!' said Turco proudly and drained the last of his beer.

'And you felt sorry for the poor mugs connected with the real winners so you decided to pay them, anonymously, what they would have won in prize money.'

'Only fair!'

'And did you ever allow for disappointment, or for bets lost, or for the poor punters who keep the show going?'

'They'd put it down to luck, Eddie. They have photos going against them every day.'

'So you didn't think beyond that? All that high tech brain power and you couldn't think beyond that? Not even about how simple it would be for someone like me to spot the routine of compensation and draw the obvious conclusion that one of your people was delivering the cash by hand?'

Turco looked puzzled and slightly hurt. 'I didn't think the jocks would talk. Cash money. Hand-delivered, no audit trail, no postmarks. How were they to know it was a one-off? There might have been a delivery every month.'

Shaking his head slowly, Eddie went to the fridge. He handed Turco a beer. 'Settle back, Ben, because I'm going to tell *you* a little story now, about a trainer called Matt Nash, and the trouble you got him into.'

TWENTY-TWO

Kim Oliver found the atmosphere in the breakfast room like a hothouse. The refectory they called it, this place with the long tables, the hard shiny floor and white walls; with its cloying fatty cooking smells, dismal adults and pale children who were unruly or silent and still as dummies.

Kim chewed and drank tea from a brown mug, resisting the temptation to dip the toast in the tea as he usually did, not wanting to do anything here he would normally do at home, determined to leave no part of his personality behind.

He gazed at the windows: ten in this high-walled room, the lower sill of each more than six feet off the floor. Easily reachable by dragging a chair or table over but he couldn't see if they were locked. Once morning classes broke for lunch, he'd try to wander around as much of the building as possible to look for the best way out. That thought set Kim off dreaming again of the farm and how big it would be, and, for what seemed a long time, he drifted off to the hills again.

Slowly he became aware of an adult standing close by him at the table. Kim looked up to see the tall, thin, grey-haired, stern-faced Mr Young staring down at him. 'Come with me, Kim, please.'

They went to the same office Kim had been brought to on the first day: small, dingy, soulless and, like the refectory, overheated. Seated by a desk was a man around the same age as Kim's father. He had the same hair colour too and a similar nose. Different coloured eyes and more of a forehead but the sight of him gave

Kim's heart a curious lift and the boy watched him get up and come smiling toward him to offer his hand.

'Kim, my name is Campbell Ogilvie, I'm a solicitor who did some work for your father.'

Shaking Mr Ogilvie's hand Kim felt suddenly grown up and responsible, ready to discuss the business of the farm. Then just as suddenly he felt awkward and stupid for thinking like that and his face reddened as he lowered his eyes and sat down in the hard upright chair Mr Young had slid toward him.

'Kim?'

Kim looked up again to see Mr Ogilvie gazing even more kindly at him. He seemed a nice man, the first decent one he'd met since the helicopter crew. Mr Ogilvie went on, 'Kim, I was so sorry to hear about your tragic news. I knew your parents well. They were good people, and I know how proud they were of you, I've come here today to tell you about those plans and the provisions your parents made for the future.'

Provisions. Future. Maybe he wouldn't have to run away after all. He watched the solicitor, who leaned forward on his chair, elbows on knees, fingertips touching. 'Once the insurance policy payments come through there will be enough money to let you complete your education at a very good boarding school and then go on to university.' Mr Ogilvie watched for Kim's reaction but the dark haired boy sat staring intently, knowing there was more.

Ogilvie cleared his throat. 'I'm afraid that the farm is to be sold, Kim.'

The farm is to be sold.

The message reverberated inside his skull. He could find nothing to say, but words came out unbidden. 'You can't sell the farm.'

Mr Ogilvie reddened. 'Kim, I'm sorry, but there is nobody to run the place, nothing to ...'

'I'll run it, sir! I'll look after it.' Kim got off the chair, feet splayed, hands apart, pleading.

Mr Ogilvie shook his head. 'Kim, you can't. I'm sorry, you're too young.'

'But I can do it! Please, I can do it! I've done it before.'

'I know how capable you are, Kim, but I'm afraid the law simply wouldn't allow it. Look, the money from the sale will be put in trust for you until you are twenty-one. Maybe then you can buy the farm back. Interest will have accrued. You could well be in a position to buy it back if you still wanted to.'

Kim fought tears of frustration and clenched his fists in anguish, and Mr Ogilvie glanced at Mr Young and was disgusted to see a smirk of enjoyment on the man's face. Ogilvie stood up. 'Please leave us alone for a few minutes.'

Young seemed surprised and half rose from his chair. 'But I'm supposed to …'

'Please give us some privacy. I have some more personal news for Kim.'

Young scowled and left. Kim stood, shoulders drooping, head down, and resolved not to raise it until his eyes had cleared. Mr Ogilvie reached forward and put his right hand softly on Kim's shoulder. 'Believe me, Kim, and believe in yourself. The next nine years will pass quickly. You'll be able to buy the farm back if you want it badly enough.'

Kim edged away and sat down. Campbell Ogilvie watched with a wretchedness of his own as he tried to decide whether to tell Kim the other piece of news. Information that would give the boy renewed hope or finish him off completely. It had been the most harrowing week Kim was ever likely to face, and Ogilvie found the situation distressing.

The solicitor had a professional duty to complete his task by telling Kim everything before leaving, but he didn't feel able to test the boy's spirit further. What he had to say would only have helped prepare Kim for betrayal or redemption; Ogilvie himself still did not know. He wouldn't find out for a few days so it was probably best, he convinced himself, to leave it until the formal decision came.

TWENTY-THREE

Being caught by Eddie was, in some ways, a relief to Ben Turco, who was bored with the photo-finish scam, and eager to find some other way of fleecing his old enemies. Eddie had called yesterday to discuss how to arrange a compensation payment to Matt Nash. Turco agreed to pay Matt £25,000 if Eddie kept quiet about the scam.

Eddie added another condition: Turco must stop the photo-finish con immediately and swear off further fraud in racing.

Turco agreed the deal. He'd already thought up a new scheme, and this time he'd leave Phil Grimond out. He'd had Grimond checked before inviting him to be at the sharp end of the photo-finish plot, but the guy turned on them with that stupid demand for two more. Well, now he didn't have a choice. Eddie had made sure of that.

Turco travelled to meet Grimond at a service station on the M1 in Northamptonshire. He swung into the car park through the dirty slush of early December. The clouds looked as though they might be ready to snow some more.

Turco had never known so much of it before January, and wondered if he should be betting on a white Christmas. This set him puzzling on the creation of a machine that could stimulate an inch of snow to fall on the roof of the London Weather Centre - the bookies' yardstick for paying out. What a coup that would be! Imagine if he could put snow there and not a flake anywhere else in London.

He resolved to give it serious thought.

Grimond slurped soup as he waited for Turco. The fat man wore the clothes he'd had on at their last meeting: tan suit and blue shirt, top button still missing.

Turco eased off his brown cord jacket with the broad fake fur lapels then rolled up the sleeves of his crimson rugby shirt. He smiled at Grimond. 'Hot in here.'

Grimond scowled and grunted as he spooned the last of the soup under his moustache. He slid the empty bowl away from him and splashed tea into a mug. He washed the tea round his mouth before swallowing then looked at the thin figure smiling falsely at him. 'What dates have you got?' Grimond asked.

'For what?'

'For the next two hits?'

'None.'

'None?'

'No dates. Nothing. It's all over. We've been rumbled, as they say.' Turco found it tough to keep the spark of mischief from his eyes. He told Grimond about Eddie.

When he finished Grimond stared at him for a while as though he despised the American for trying to fool him. 'You're a liar.'

Turco reached into his jacket pocket and pulled out a mobile phone. He pressed then held it up so Grimond could see Eddie's name. Turco slid it across the grey tabletop. 'Why don't you ask him yourself?'

Grimond, unsure now, looked at the phone then stared unblinking at Turco, who met his gaze. After what seemed a long time Grimond pushed the phone back across and said, 'I'll handle Malloy, you just sort out the next dates.'

Turco half laughed. 'What do you mean *handle* him? You're kidding! Eddie is smart and he's tough. Be thankful he's offered us the easy way out.'

'Too easy. Eddie might know, but you must have told him. Just to try and get me out of the picture.'

Turco raised his eyes and sighed in frustration. 'Look, Phil, there's no picture left, which doesn't mean we stuck the frame around you. Eddie found out because he was smarter than us. He's keeping quiet because I've agreed to pay off some of the people who suffered. Now, can we just drop the whole thing and roll on home?'

'You roll on home, cowboy, and work out the next date with your partners. Leave Malloy to me. He won't interfere.'

In the family house at the Malloy stud in Newmarket, Marie came downstairs for the twentieth time that day, after checking on her bed-bound mother. She sat at the kitchen table and reached for the pink mug, half full of cooling coffee. Her fingers stayed on the handle as her mind drifted through the years to when her mother used to be the one always checking on the daughter.

The riflecrack sound of the letterbox being pushed roughly open snapped her back to the present and, still seated in the kitchen, Marie watched a sheave of mail fall into the wire basket behind the door.

'Various shades of brown,' she muttered to herself as she went to collect the day's bills. On top of the pile was a yellow envelope with a Carlisle postmark. It was addressed to her, redirected from her old house, the one she'd sold to move in with her mother.

The heavy franking mark read 'Ogilvie, Speed and Minto, Solicitors'.

Did she know that name, that company? Something about it sparked a tiny light in the tunnel of her memory. She sat down. She opened the envelope and her past unfolded with the letter. Four neat paragraphs on elegant cream paper. Four hammer blows taking her back to the time of her fascination with the coal-fired forge her father used to work. Watching him toil hard-faced among the sparks, Marie had formed her first adult metaphor: life was an anvil and fate wielded the hammer; you never knew when the next blow would fall, how hard it would be, or how it would reshape you.

TWENTY-FOUR

Rather than make his daily phone call to check on Matt Nash, Eddie drove to Lambourn to give him the good news in person.

'Twenty-five grand? For nothing?'

'Hardly for nothing.' Eddie pointed to Matt's hand resting beside the mug of coffee on the pine table. The trainer looked down, moving the still scabbed fingers and thumb. 'I sometimes just sit and move my fingers, you know. For ages. Spreading them, tapping this half-one like a sawn-off drumstick. I've developed a morbid fascination with them.'

Eddie sipped coffee. Matt looked again at his battered hand. 'Funny to think they've been with you all your life,' he said. 'Fingers, I mean. Remember when they used to be like little claws, when you were a baby? Tiny. Like twigs. Easily snapped.'

Eddie shrugged. 'Can't say I've thought that much about it.'

Matt kept moving them, opening and closing, rhythmically, watching.

'Drink your coffee,' Eddie said.

Matt's hand moved to the blue mug and his fingers closed slowly around it. 'Sometimes it's like they've got a life of their own,' he said.

'You've been living alone too long, my friend. Get a wife.'

'Ha! I've had three. Keep losing them. If you hadn't burst into that cellar when you did, I might well be sitting here now with more ex-wives than fingers. Or more ex-fingers than ex-wives, if you wanted to look at it that way.'

'Your mind is working in mysterious ways, Matt.'

He looked again at his hand. 'I think I'm marginally still sane. Marginally.'

Eddie watched him. 'More than can be said for many. Maybe it's time to try and forget it all now. I take it you've heard nothing more from them?'

'The chinks? Not a whisper. Strange.'

'Not strange, really. Most bullies act the same. When somebody stands up to them, they slither away to find another victim.'

'Trouble is, it wasn't me who did the standing up.'

'Listen, you toughed it out without breaking or conceding anything while they were trying to mince your fingers. Don't knock yourself. It's easy for me to come barrelling in on the back of a major tantrum. You'd have done the same in my position.'

'I'd like to think I would, but I know I wouldn't. If you'd been counting on me, you'd be sitting there fingerless, my friend. Can you imagine what you'd have been like now handling reins?'

Eddie laughed. So did Matt as he rose to rinse his coffee mug. 'Want something stronger, Eddie?'

'Nah. I'll be heading back soon. Heard anything from Rebecca?'

'Fancy her, do you?'

'Not if I'm tramping on anybody's fingers...er, I mean toes.'

'Very funny. Well you've got no worries about that. Becky and I are just business partners.'

Eddie looked at him. 'I didn't know that.'

Matt smiled. 'I don't have to tell you everything, do I?'

'Business partners in the yard, you mean?'

'Not strictly. Becky sent me two horses and I'm training them for nothing until her twenty-fifth birthday when she gets another million from daddy's trust fund.'

'Nice. When's the birthday?'

'March 17th, Gold Cup day.' Matt drew on his forehead with his half-finger. 'Etched in my brain. Prince Simba wins the Gold Cup and Becky Bow gets her million.'

'And then what? If you don't mind me asking.'

'Then Miss Bow buys another half-dozen horses and a half share in the yard. And we all live happily ever after. At least that's what it says in my book.'

'Life and How to Live It?'

73

'That's the one. By Matt Nash. The man who put the opt in optimism.'

TWENTY-FIVE

On Wednesday, Kim rose early and ironed the only white shirt he had. He showered and combed his thick dark hair, still damp from washing. Kim checked himself in the oval plastic-framed mirror in his room. It was important to look as mature as possible. He wanted the adults to start taking him seriously. In the midday break, he walked along the gloomy corridor toward Mr Young's office.

Ten paces from it, Kim heard the outside door close and a few seconds later Mr Ogilvie came into view. They stopped and looked at each other. Mr Ogilvie smiled and said, 'Kim, good morning.'

'Good morning, sir. I was just going to ask Mr Young if I could see you.'

'Now that's a coincidence, Kim, because I've come to see you again anyway. If you don't mind waiting a second I'll just let Mr Young know I've arrived.'

Kim nodded, gazing at Ogilvie as he knocked on the office door. The solicitor seemed on edge. Kim wondered if something had happened. Maybe the insurance company wasn't going to pay out after all. Or they'd already found a buyer for the farm. His mind raced looking for other potential disasters.

The office door opened and Mr Young came out smiling. He said to Kim, 'Mr Ogilvie wishes to speak to you again.' He stepped to the side, holding an arm outstretched to usher Kim in.

Kim was relieved when Mr Young pulled the door closed leaving him alone in the room with Mr Ogilvie who'd removed his coat to reveal a tweed suit over a mustard coloured shirt and brown tie. He crossed his legs and Kim noticed the heavy brown brogues. Mr Ogilvie had big feet. He asked Kim to sit down. Kim chose the same chair as yesterday but tried to sit straighter in it, taller.

Ogilvie's smile faded and his voice sounded tense. 'Kim, I have some more news for you which I've just received this morning.' He picked up the soft leather briefcase, undid the buckle then reconsidered. What was the point of pulling out the fax? He'd only be using it as a prop.

He put the case down again and said, 'Kim, I realize there could be no bigger shock to you than the dreadful thing that happened to your father, but I have something to tell you that you may find distressing. That ... that you will find distressing.'

Kim swallowed involuntarily and felt his mouth go dry.

'Kim, I've got to tell you that your mum and dad were not your biological parents.'

Kim stared at him. Ogilvie continued, 'Your mum and dad adopted you at birth. They couldn't have children of their own and this made you extra special to them. I know this. I'd known them both from before you were born.'

Kim replayed these words, trying to make them sink in, but something told him Mr Ogilvie had the wrong person, that he'd come to the wrong children's home. Kim had had his share of bad luck, surely this was someone else's, mistakenly delivered to him.

Ogilvie watched him. 'Kim, do you understand what I'm saying?'

Kim nodded vaguely. His mouth had dropped open an inch.

Ogilvie said, 'I know it must be desperately difficult for you to take in and perhaps I should have warned you yesterday but I was waiting for one more link in the chain and I received that, so to speak, this morning.' He paused to draw a long breath then interlocked his fingers and leaned further forward. Kim watched now as though hypnotized.

'Your mother and father made separate Wills, Kim, and both specifically requested that should something like this happen, this terrible tragedy, that I should act on their behalf and contact your biological mother to offer her the chance to, to renew...to take over...'

'To have me back?' Kim offered quietly.

'Yes. In effect.' Ogilvie felt his scalp prickle with sweat.

Kim said, 'And she doesn't want me.' A statement.

Ogilvie cleared his throat. 'Her family circumstances are very difficult, Kim. I wish I could tell you more, but I'm restricted by confidentiality. If I were able to explain things in more detail, I think you would find everything easier to understand. I'm sorry.'

Kim sat half-stooped now, staring at his shoes.

'Was my mother a single mother? Did he leave her? Is that why she had to give me away?'

'I'm sorry, Kim. There are rules I must follow. Rules that I hate sometimes. Rules I'd love to break. But I can't.'

'Can you tell me her name?'

'I'm sorry, I can't. It wouldn't be ethical and it wouldn't help you in the long run. Believe me.'

'Where does she live, then? Can you tell me that?'

'No, I'm afraid I can tell you absolutely nothing about her. Your mum and dad made an agreement with her when you were born and that cannot be broken.'

'But Mum and Dad are dead. Does my real Mum know that?'

Another deep breath. 'Yes, she does.'

Kim stared at the floor. Ogilvie writhed inside as he watched the boy swallow lumps in his throat.

'And she still doesn't want me. Won't she even see me, just for an hour or something? Half an hour?'

The lawyer shook his head.

Kim put his hands together. He shrugged and Ogilvie read that gesture as one of forced adult acceptance. But the boy's head drooped, then hung loose so that he went from looking at the floor to looking beneath the chair he sat on.

Ogilvie leaned forward and rested a hand on Kim's shoulder. 'Perhaps someday, your mother's circumstances will change,' he said quietly.

Kim silently forced all the air out of his lungs and closed his eyes and wondered how long he could wait until he had to take a breath.

TWENTY-SIX

Back home after a fruitless day at Ludlow, Eddie dumped his kit bag in the kitchen, made coffee and called Ben Turco whose voice boomed and echoed down the line. Eddie said, 'You sound like you're in a cathedral.'

'The cathedral of dreams, Eddie, the cathedral of high technology. Would you believe I am two rooms from where the telephone is?'

'I'd believe you're two rooms short of a full apartment.'

'Excuse me?'

'Forget it. You wanted to speak to me?'

'Yes.' Still the big echo.

'Ben, do me a favour? Get to the phone and pick it up. I feel like I'm talking to God.'

'You almost are! Only kidding! Jesus, that's blasphemy.'

A few seconds later Turco's voice sounded normal. 'I called to warn you about Phil Grimond - you know, the guy who was in with us?'

'The photo finish operator?'

'That's him. I spoke to him this morning, told him you knew, so we didn't have any choice but to pack up, but he wasn't having it. He said I should sort out the next date and let him deal with you.'

Eddie thought for a few seconds then said, 'Why does Grimond actually need you? If he's got the computer chip or whatever it is, why doesn't he just find himself another partner to help him run the scam?'

'Ah, well now… !' Eddie could hear Turco smiling. 'Do you think Ben Turco would let go control of that baby? The system won't authorise until I send it a signal via satellite. No one can run it without my co-operation.'

'Okay. What did Grimond mean when he said he'd deal with me?'

'He didn't elaborate but I don't think his intentions are honourable.'

'So how did you leave it? Is he expecting you to carry on, to give him another date?'

'He's a greedy man, Eddie, and he's desperate. It wouldn't surprise me if he's in with some people he can't handle, some guys out of his league. Maybe it's them who're putting the pressure on him to set up another one.'

'But how could he have tied anyone else into the photo finish con? He never knew what race it would be, if any. There's obviously no way of predicting whether or not a race will end in a photo.'

'But if it did, and we were operating on it, he'd only have to tell his confederates to keep an eye on Magnus and see if he started betting on the outcome. Then they'd just follow him in.'

'True. I hadn't thought of that.'

'So, Edward, the problem remains. What do we do about Grimond?'

'I don't know. McCarthy's away for a few days. He's promised to meet me as soon as he gets back, which I think is on Friday. I can easily mention Grimond and still keep you out of it. You've given the guy a chance to pull out and get clear. If Grimond chooses not to then I wouldn't feel any obligation to him. Let the Jockey Club Security guys nail him if they can, though they're not the brightest bunch around.'

'So why don't we help them along a little bit?'

'How?'

'Set him up. Tell him there's another job on, authorise the chip then have those security guys bust in on him.'

'Wouldn't he try to drop you in it, then?'

'He could try all he wanted but there's no way he'd be able to prove it.'

'You're sure?'

'Positive. I'd take my chances for the sake of getting rid.'

'Okay. How do we play it?'

'Just how I said. We only need to work out the details.'

'Just bear in mind McCarthy will need about a week's notice to get his team in gear.'

'Okay. See you soon.'

'Ben, can you arrange another transfer into my bank account? Five grand should do.'

'Operating expenses?'

'Payment of a debt from you to Laura Gilpin, the woman who trains Samson's Curls.'

'She got her money! Walter delivered it!'

'Walter tried to, remember? Trouble was he dropped into my place first and never got any further.'

'Oh! ... I forgot about that. Okay, no problem. When are you seeing Miss Gilpin?'

'She has a horse entered at Catterick tomorrow. She'll be there.'

'Fine.'

'Right. See you.'

'Eddie!'

'Uhuh?'

'Tell Miss Gilpin I'm sorry, will you? Anonymously?'

'I will.'

TWENTY-SEVEN

The soft hills and meadowlands of Shropshire, where Eddie was based, close to the Welsh border, seemed shaped to deflect the worst of winter's gales. Eddie noticed how much colder it seemed in the east, where the Yorkshire landscape invited in the slicing wind, to toughen its natives and deter incomers. Eddie shivered as he grabbed his kitbag from the car and made for the warmth of the Catterick weighing room. The first race was two hours off, but the newspaper sellers, bookmakers, police and catering staff filtered in slowly; no cause for excitement on this bread-and-butter racing day.

As Eddie approached the exit from the car park, he heard a shout and turned to see the unmistakable figure of Tiny Delaware lumbering toward him. Tiny stood six feet seven and must have weighed thirty stone. Although fat-bellied he had huge broad shoulders and a barrel chest. Eddie considered him a modern version of a fairy-tale giant.

Tiny always wore a knee-length, tan, canvas-type coat, its many stains like maps on a parchment. Then there was the big white Stetson and the tartan kipper tie. He'd been bumming around the tracks for as long as Eddie could remember, one of a handful of offbeat characters the sport seemed to attract.

Eddie smiled, waiting to feel the ground shake, as Tiny hurried forward. He began slowing down about ten yards away and pulled himself to a halt in front of Eddie. 'How you doing, Tiny?'

'Brilliant, Eddie! Great! The past week has been the best of my life ...' He was panting. Eddie waited. Tiny, red-cheeked under the shade of the Stetson, went on '... came at the right time too with Christmas round the corner.'

'Good. Good for you,' Eddie said, knowing Tiny would lose the lot by the weekend, never mind by Christmas. 'What can I do for you, Tiny?'

Perplexed, the big man fished deep in his trouser pockets. 'Eddie, I'm sorry, I didn't mean to delay you. Won't keep you a few seconds actually, if I can just...' He dug deeper. 'Tell you what it is, I bought my little nephew an autograph book for Christmas and he's racing mad, bonkers ... where is the bloody thing? I thought I'd ask you to sign it, Eddie, if you don't mind. I want to get a few jockeys and trainers in it for him. Be a lovely surprise.'

'Of course I will. No problem.'

'Great. You'll be the first in it. If I can find it. Bloody typical, isn't it?' Tiny groped at the outside of his coat below the pocket, squeezing with his right hand. His face lit up in satisfaction and he opened the coat to reach inside a poacher's pocket. Eddie watched him pull out banded bundles of ten and twenty pound notes, which he tried to balance in the crook of his arm.

Eddie said, 'You have had a good week. You weren't kidding.'

Tiny smiled wide. 'Small change!' Still pulling out wads of cash, he gave three bundles to Eddie. 'Here, hold this a minute, I'm near the bottom now!' Eddie held the cash and took two more before Tiny found the autograph book and handed it to him, taking back the money.

Eddie reached into his jacket for a pen. 'What's the boy's name?'

'Matthew, it is. That would be great, Eddie, if you could put, to Matthew with best wishes.'

Eddie wrote on the first page of the thick leather-bound book and gave it to Tiny with a smile.

'Brilliant, Eddie, thanks a lot! Now, what do you know today?'

'I know you'll probably lose that cash unless you keep it in your pocket.'

Tiny smiled. 'No chance. I'll be putting half of it on the hotpot you ride in the second.'

'It'll be odds-on, Tiny, you should never bet odds on when they've got eight obstacles to jump.'

'Nah, he's different class. See you in the winner's enclosure.'

'Well, I hope so.' Eddie turned to head through the entrance.

Tiny said, 'Come on, I'll walk in with you.' And they ambled into the course, Tiny slipping an arm round Eddie's shoulder and leaning low to pump him for more information.

With no ride in the first, Eddie sat in the weighing room catching up on the gossip among the northern jockeys. There was no talk of Turco's racket.

In the second race, Eddie rode the hot favourite, Keelhaul, going for its fourth win in a row. An unbeaten novice hurdler, Eddie had ridden it in all three victories and today it was long odds-on to beat much inferior opposition.

When Keelhaul's trainer legged him up into the saddle, Eddie prepared for the usual jinking and jogging. The narrow, almost black horse was an edgy type, all nervous energy, a natural front-runner who couldn't wait to get on with things. But the horse stood still as Eddie slipped his toes into the stirrups and gathered the reins. Pleasantly surprised, Eddie smiled down at Keelhaul's lad. 'You been sending him to transcendental meditation classes?' The lad looked puzzled then gave an embarrassed shrug and tugged on the bridle. Keelhaul ambled off as the trainer gripped the half-folded blanket, letting his horse walk from under it. The lad unclipped his lead rein and let Keelhaul go.

As he reached the course, Eddie curled his tongue and gave an encouraging clicking sound and Keelhaul lurched into a reluctant canter.

Eddie couldn't make his mind up if Keelhaul had grown up a bit, or was off colour. He moved to the start lethargically, but not so poorly as to prompt Eddie to ask the starter to look at him. He was definitely sound and, anyway, he'd only need to be half-right to beat this lot.

Eddie lined up next to the inside rail, Keelhaul's white blazed head just inches from the starting tape, which rattled in the wind. The horse never flinched at the noise even though the grey beside him spooked and spun round, barging into three others.

When the tapes rose, Keelhaul led for the first two hurdles, but he was labouring and Eddie knew the horse would do well to finish, let alone win.

Despite a few sharp cracks from Eddie's whip, Keelhaul slowly lost ground to drop away among the tail enders.

On a horse with no obvious chance, toiling with the also rans wouldn't have been so bad. But Keelhaul was a very hot favourite.

Eddie had a ride in the next and needed to get back as quickly as possible. That stopped him pulling up and, as sometimes happens, the breather seemed to do the trick. Keelhaul passed several horses and kept galloping.

The leaders were gone, leaving a twenty length gap to the next bunch, with Keelhaul now rapidly closing on them, though too far off the action to have any chance. Not wanting to give his mount a hard time for nothing, Eddie eased him through the tired and backward horses to run on into fifth place, twelve lengths behind the winner. Keelhaul pulled up fresher than when the race started, and Eddie knew questions would be asked about the ride. The stewards' Inquiry announcement blared out before he dismounted beside an angry trainer and dejected owners.

None seemed convinced by his explanation and Eddie walked away cradling his saddle and shaking his head. He ignored the gibes of losing punters. He understood how they felt, but there was nothing he could tell them that would make things better. Some of the name-calling grew crude, tempting him to turn on the crowd, but he forced himself to walk on toward the weighing room.

Perhaps Keelhaul would cough on the way home or when having a bite of grass. Maybe later his lad would spot the tell-tale signs of blood in the nostrils that would indicate a broken blood vessel.

That was all Eddie could suggest to the stewards; the explanation that there was no explanation. They heard from the starter who confirmed that the gelding had been unusually subdued. The trainer declared himself "baffled".

The stewards 'noted' Eddie's comments, which meant they didn't quite believe him but, for the moment, couldn't prove anything else. Eddie's mood worsened as he left the stewards' room. He went straight outside in the perverse hope that some of those punters who'd barracked him might still be around.

He stood leaning on the fence glowering at the few passers-by.

'Hey, you! Malloy!'

Teeth clenched, eyes blazing, he spun to see the large figure of Laura Gilpin walking toward him. She smiled warmly but when she saw his face, her eyes opened wide and she held out her palm at arm's length, as though warding him off, though she kept coming.

She laughed nervously and said, 'Calm down! I was only joking! Jeez, if looks could kill. I'm sorry.'

He cooled quickly as he saw the funny side. 'You nearly got a real mouthful then, Laura,' he said.

'As the Bishop said to the actress.' Her cheeks were rosy, her eyes bright and happy. 'Did they give you a tough time in there?'

'You're certain they don't believe you, know what I mean?' She nodded, impressed by Eddie's anger. Face animated and hands expressive he went on, 'They don't even try to hide it. They just sit staring and their eyes are saying, "We're sure you're bent, Malloy. We only wish we could prove it." It makes you want to get in close, make them stand up face to face, one on one. They haven't a fucking clue.'

Laura watched, attracted by his fiery attitude, amused by the hurt look. She became aware of him looking at her as though expecting an answer, but she hadn't taken in the last few things he'd said. She smiled wider and guessed. 'Don't worry, tomorrow's another day,' she said.

Eddie frowned in puzzlement. 'What?'

Laura owned up. 'I'm sorry, I wasn't listening. Too caught up in watching you be Mister Angry. What did you say?'

'I said I've got something for you.'

'Animal, vegetable or mineral?'

'Collateral.'

'In the form of?'

'That rare modern day commodity, cash.'

'I'm all ears. And pockets.'

'Well, as good as cash. A very solid cheque.'

'From whom?'

'From the man who made you cry at Ascot.'

Laura looked puzzled. Eddie said, 'Can you meet me after the last and I'll tell you all about it?'

'Oh come on, Eddie, that's hours away! You can't hang me out then just walk off.'

He smiled. 'Sorry, I'm riding in the next. See you later.'

Laura clenched her fists and stamped in mock frustration. Eddie laughed and went into the weighing room.

Eddie rode a winner in the third, and Laura Gilpin's only runner at the meeting finished second. They met again as arranged, and went to a small half-full bar at the end of the stand.

They sat by the steamed-up window. Eddie watched Laura make baby footprints in the condensation with the side of her clenched fist and her fingertip. She was determined not to beg for what he'd promised, and he played on it, making small talk until she finally banged theatrically on the table and said, 'Oh, come on, tell me! Tell me!'

He laughed. She smiled and he reached to the floor and opened his kitbag to take out his cheque book. He wrote her a cheque for £5,000 and held it out. 'From a fan of yours who wanted to ease your disappointment over Samson's Curls'.

She laid the cheque on the tabletop and looked at it. 'The man who made me cry at Ascot. Tell me more.'

Eddie shrugged. 'He says to tell you he's sorry.'

'For what?'

'Your loss.'

'Conscience money.'

'Yes.'

'How did he do it?'

Eddie leaned across the table. 'The cheque is clean and above board. You can take it without a worry. I wish I could tell you more about it but I can't.'

She pushed the corner of the cheque under a beer mat. 'How did he fiddle the photo?'

'I can't tell you anything.'

'How did you catch him?'

'Laura, look, bank the cheque, honestly…'

'Don't worry, I'm banking it. I just want the story behind it. I'm a Gemini. Curiosity's my driving force.'

'Well I'm a Taurus. Obstinacy's mine.'

She relaxed in her chair, drank some whiskey and stared at Eddie over the glass. 'Oh well, I suppose I'll have to ask around. I'm sure the grapevine will be carrying it soon.'

'Please don't do that.'

'Why?' She smiled.

'As a favour to me. It's not done with yet. I'll tell you more when it is.'

They held each other's gaze, then she reached across the table. Eddie smiled and shook her hand. She picked up the cheque.

Through the fading light they walked to the car park, Laura's thirteen stone bulk under her long coat exaggerating Eddie's slimness in his dark suit. She asked if he thought she should enter Samson's Curls at Cheltenham in ten days. He said she should and agreed to ride it.

They stopped at Eddie's car. A dozen vehicles dotted the car park. Standing beside a silver estate car near the exit, Eddie noticed the huge figure of Tiny Delaware handing a man bundles of cash. Eddie reckoned it must be a bookie, and he wondered what Tiny planned to use now to buy his Christmas presents. He told Laura about his conversation with Tiny and, getting into his car, said, 'Let that be a lesson to you to keep that five grand in your cleavage. The bookies always win.'

'You think my cleavage would hold five grand? It must be a better view from on top of those horses than I thought.'

Eddie laughed. 'Figuratively speaking.'

'Yes, my figure. I think I'd stash two-and-half in each cup. Maintain good balance. Leave the cleavage free for ventilation.'

'Well, if you need a hand to stack it, let me know.'

'I'll slot you into the waiting list.'

He smiled. 'Do that.'

'See you. Drive safely. Keep your eyes on the road and your mind on the job.' Laura pushed his door closed and watched him pull away. She wandered off, smiling, in the direction of the horsebox park. She took the cheque from her pocket as she walked. She sniffed it, then unbuttoned her blouse and folded it into her cleavage. She held out her arms, still walking through the dusk, shaking out her hair and saying in a fake sultry voice, 'Come and get it Mister M. Come and get it!'

TWENTY-EIGHT

At 6.30pm, Kim finished a game of table tennis and told the others he was going to his room to read. What few clothes he had, along with a spare pair of shoes, his toothbrush and shampoo had been fitted into two plastic carriers, which Kim found easy to push through the upper window in the bathroom at the end of the hall. Climbing to stand on the sink he got a knee onto the white-tiled sill and wriggled through, pale blue paint flakes from the ledge sticking to his thick black sweater.

Kim dropped silently to the ground, rose to a half crouch, senses at animal pitch. No shouts. No footsteps coming after him. He gathered his bags and scurried through the sparse trees in the acre of grounds that surrounded the home. No fence to negotiate, just a low stone wall fronting a thick hedge. Kim found a gap, and a few broken twigs joined the paint flakes on his sweater.

On the pavement underneath the orange street lamps his breath mingled with the cold mist. No noise. No traffic. Down the hill he could hear a stream burbling over rocks. He decided to find the stream and follow it for a while before coming back onto the streets.

By eight o'clock he'd been waiting by a slip road on the M6 for half an hour and the cold was in his bones. Underneath the sweater he wore a hooded white sweatshirt that he tucked into his blue jeans to try and keep some warmth. He'd been optimistic about getting a lift to Penrith, certain that a friendly lorry driver would stop for him, but they'd all gone whizzing past as though they didn't care or hadn't even seen him.

Hadn't seen him.

Kim wondered about the dark clothes he wore. Shivering, he stripped off his tops and reversed the order, pulling the white sweatshirt on over the black jumper. Within ten minutes, he sat in the warmth of a big lorry cab telling the driver he planned to pay his mum a surprise visit.

Three and a half hours and two lifts later Kim stood on the closest main road to the farm, a six-mile-walk away. Swinging his bags and whistling, Kim set off along the narrow track leading west knowing he was nearly home.

Eddie ate a light dinner with Charles Tunney, his trainer, and afterward, drinking by the fire, they spread paperwork on the yew-topped coffee table and made plans for runners over the coming month. Many of Charles's horses had been out of sorts, but they were showing signs of returning to form. Eddie wouldn't have to graft so hard for rides elsewhere now.

Racing yards sometimes move in and out of form in the way athletes do. Nobody knows what brings the hot streaks, or how long they'll last. But they happen, and along with them comes confidence for all: trainer, stable-jockey, grooms, secretary, head lad…confidence, good cheer, money from winning bets and a shot of immunity against the bad times…an optimism reload.

Charles also told Eddie he'd be going to Ireland to see four new horses.

They had three runners at Leicester the following day and Eddie would be up extra early to school six over fences before breakfast. Charles was on his third whiskey and his tenth daydream when Eddie left him to it and headed across the darkened yard to his flat. Ben Turco had left a message on the answerphone. Eddie called him.

'What can I do for you?'

'Cheltenham, a week Saturday. How does that sound for setting up Grimond?'

'It sounds okay to me. It'll depend on McCarthy.'

'Is that time enough to get his boys moving?'

'Should be. I'll try and reach him tomorrow.'

'Good. I'll start finalizing arrangements.'

'Is there anything I have to do?'

'Nope. Leave it all to me.'

'Okay.'

'One thing for you to think about, Eddie, you know that stuff you do for *The Racing Channel?*'

'The studio guest thing?'

'Yeah, where you go in for a day and spout comments on runners, give tips and stuff. Do you have full access to the studio where the live broadcast goes out from?'

'Why are you asking?'

'Because I've an idea which is probably the most brilliant thing I've ever come up with.'

'If you say so yourself.'

'If I say so myself! It would make you a rich man.'

'And what would it make you, Ben?'

'Richer. I'm already rich. Richer.'

'By how much?'

'Millions.'

'Dollars?'

'Whatever. Why? You interested?'

'How crooked is it?'

'That depends on where you're standing.'

'Well, let's say I'm standing outside the dock and want to stay there.'

Turco cleared his throat. 'The main victims would be the bookies and they deserve everything life throws their way. No mercy.'

'And who would the other victims be?'

'A few punters might lose, but the same number would probably win. And even the ones who lost would applaud the audacity of the whole thing.'

'I doubt it, somehow.'

'Don't. I don't do doubt.'

'I do do doubt.'

'Don't let it become your default position, man. There's more to life.'

'So I hear.'

'Eddie, honestly. I've never known a sport like racing for people to desert the world.'

'Ben…what are you talking about? If you're dipping into your philosophy degree for the next part of this conversation, just talk while I go and put the kettle on.'

'Seriously. You guys get so wrapped up in horses, everything else that happens on the planet might as well be happening on another planet. When you lie down tonight, instead of riding tomorrow's races in your head ten times over, think about what you could do with five million sterling.'

'Save it, Ben. I don't want to know.' Eddie ran a weary hand through his hair and glanced at the window as fat blobs of rain splatted against the pane.

'Eddie, gimme a chance to explain it properly. Come down and see me. We'll have dinner. Take in a show.'

Eddie sighed, 'It'd have to be some show to beat you for entertainment. I'm not interested in any of your scams, Ben. Let's sort Grimond out so I can get on with riding.'

'We could pull this off easily if your access to *The Racing Channel* studio also gets us into the full SiS bag. I'm telling you, you'd never have to ride again in your life. Just think, no more rainy Hexhams, no marathon trips to Plumpton, the end of swinging your leg over raw novices and hoping you don't come back paralyzed, no more—'

'Goodnight, Ben.'

'Eddie! Hear me out, please, you owe it to yourself.'

'Oh don't give me that bullshit, for God's sake! Look, I'm tired. I'll speak to McCarthy in the morning about Cheltenham. I'll be in touch. Goodnight.' He hung up and stood for a minute listening to the rain on the window pane. He undressed by lamplight then brushed his teeth, scouring out the remaining morsels of the fillet steak dinner.

He lay wondering what Turco was cooking up now, marveling at the guy's inventiveness. He smiled. Turco had set him thinking about SiS. Eddie hadn't done a stint there for weeks.

SiS covered race-meetings in the UK, sending live pictures or, on busy days, an audio coverage to 10,000 betting shops. Occasionally, Eddie would appear as a studio guest, chatting about racing and offering what wisdom he could within the libel laws; an art in its own right. Eddie stretched and closed his eyes. His thoughts moved to Becky Bow, to their dinner date. He forgot about horses for a while, reflecting briefly that Ben Turco would be pleased about that.

TWENTY-NINE

For those whose business was riding National Hunt horses through an English winter, dark mornings brought frustration. Sometimes Eddie would sit at the east window waiting for the sun to deliver that first glow, hoping for a side order of warmth with his light. Enough to kill the frost. Sufficient to soften the gallops on the hill.

And this morning, he got that. Easy, squelchy ground which sucked noisily at the hooves of the chestnut mare as she raced toward her first ever fence in her maiden schooling session, blackthorn blurring on her left, white rails on her right. Aiming her at the target, Eddie changed rein, trying to get her on stride, in rhythm, shortened up, as a schoolboy long-jumper shortens approaching the take-off board. And the sodden turf served Eddie and the six-year-old mare well when she rammed the black birch halfway up with her white-stockinged front legs, firing Eddie from her back, then following him as she turned over, horse chasing human in a long tumbling skid, Eddie's narrow muddy traveling furrow being erased by the mare's wider brown swathe that was scribed by her flailing hooves, the earth slowing her, bringing her gently to a halt before she could catch and crush her jockey.

Filthy and wet, but unhurt, Eddie climbed the stairs to his flat, shedding his clothes and boots in the hallway and making for the shower, clicking the radio on as he passed and dialing up the volume. Clean clothes laid out, towel warming on the radiator, Eddie stepped into the shower as his phone rang. He cursed.

'Eddie?' It was Peter McCarthy

'Who else would it be, Mac?'

'It didn't sound like you.'

'Probably because I'm buck naked, cold and covered in mud that I got when a mare thought I'd make a better plough than a jockey.'

'You fell off.'

'Yes.'

'You're an honest man.'

'I'm a shivering man and a poor man who's getting poorer by the second as my shower spews perfectly clean, expensive hot water down the drain that I would be standing over if you hadn't called. What do you want?'

'Just to tell you I can't meet you until Monday. Sorry.'

'Monday's fine. See you then.'

As soon as the receiver settled in the cradle, it rang again. Eddie yanked it back up. 'Yes!'

'Eddie?'

'Rebecca? Sorry. Sorry, I'm having a bad morning.'

'Anything serious?'

'No, just crap timing. Couldn't see a stride when I was schooling, turned my shower on just as the phone rang, took my clothes off too soon.'

'Steady, boy! It's early in the day to be planting those pictures in my mind.'

'You'd run a mile if you saw me now.'

'Don't bet on it.'

They let the pause lengthen.

'You riding at Sandown on Saturday?'

'I am. You going?'

'I'll be there. I thought I could buy you dinner afterwards. If you've nothing better to do. And you're not insulted at a woman picking up the tab.'

'Gigolo work would suit me. Count me in.'

She laughed. 'I'll see you at the track.'

THIRTY

If it had been Eddie Malloy's intention to show off to Rebecca Bow at Sandown, then things backfired badly. On his first ride, he mistimed his run and lost a race he should have won. In the other, his horse made what looked from the stands to be only a slight mistake but it caught him napping and he fell off.

When he met her by the parade ring, he was proud to be seen with her. She wore a lime coloured silk jacket and trousers and matching shoes. Her large coin-shaped silver earrings bore some Chinese design, and she carried a small green bag of soft leather. Her blonde hair hung in a shining swathe. She sensed him beside her, turned and elegantly raised her head for Eddie to kiss her cheek. The smell of her perfume excited him.

For the rest of the day they were seldom more than a few feet apart. Eddie felt he'd redeemed himself by tipping Rebecca two winners. Her enthusiasm in cheering them home made him happy and he thought once more about Turco's advice about enjoying other things in life.

Although he tried to argue her out of it, Rebecca insisted on paying for dinner that evening from her winnings.

They found a country house hotel with a romantic restaurant, and Eddie lost track of time. They ate and talked and drank and he watched Rebecca's hazel eyes glint in the candlelight and wished that he could take her upstairs.

He found himself talking more to her than he could remember doing with anyone. As he spoke, she gazed at him as though every word was vital to her. She in turn told him things about her family, about the heartache over her father's death.

'A car crash, wasn't it?' Eddie asked.

She nodded. 'Fifty-three, he was ... Fifty-three!'

'Young.'

'He was a young man in his heart. He would always have been young, no matter what age he'd lived to, if you know what I mean.'

Eddie smiled. 'Most men never grow up.'

'Including you?'

'Especially me.'

He steered her off the subject of her father, not wanting to see her look sad. They talked about Matt and the Chinese and that night in London.

'Still got your gun?' Eddie asked.

'Tucked into my garter.'

'I wouldn't be surprised. When did you start carrying it?'

'A friend of mine gave it to me months ago. I was helping her clear out her flat and she came across it, offered it to me and I thought I might have some fun with it.'

'You had some fun with it the other night.'

She laughed and sipped white wine. 'You should have seen their eyes pop wide. Suddenly they didn't look Chinese anymore.'

Eddie smiled. 'You don't seem worried.'

'About what?'

'Revenge.'

'On me?'

'You. Matt.' He bit off the inclusion of himself.

'No chance. The boss man will find easier targets. They're not the kind of people who are used to being on the receiving end. It's not as if you left old Lee Sung in any doubt, is it? Would *you* mess with you after that?'

'I'm not a Triad boss with a reputation to protect.'

'I don't think he is, either. I think they're a squalid little bunch of moonlighters, trying to get some easy money from poor Matt.'

'Moonlighters?'

'You know, picking on the little fish to supplement whatever the Triad pays them.'

'Is that how it works?'

'What?' She pushed hair behind her ear.

'The Triads.'

'I don't know. That's how it seems to me. That's what I said to Matt.'

'And did you mean it, or were you just trying to look after him, help him sleep better?'

'You've mistaken me for an angel of mercy, Mister Malloy.' She nailed him with that intense gaze again.

'I don't think so. You look pretty angelic to me.'

She smiled. 'Matt means a lot to me. I don't like to see him scared.'

'Me neither.'

'Well, you did your bit. You're a tough guy, Eddie. That's given Matt more confidence than anything I could say or do.'

'I'm all bluff. Pretty soft really.'

'I haven't met a soft jockey yet. Met lots of crazy ones, and a couple who were as dim as two-watt light-bulbs, but I ain't met any soft ones.'

Eddie wondered how close she'd been to some of those jockeys and he felt a stab of jealousy.

The longer they talked, the more he liked her devil-may-care attitude to life.

Late on, his mind slowed and warmed by whiskey and desire, Eddie felt he should establish himself with Rebecca as something more than a brawler with a short temper and poor judgment. He steered the conversation around again to that race at Ascot and he told Rebecca the truth about what had been behind it all. He played down his role in the capture of Walter, and how he'd stopped Turco going any further, but he knew she'd suss what had happened and who the 'hero' had been.

She seemed so engrossed in his story, he drank some more and decided he should top things off by telling her about the set-up planned for Grimond.

THIRTY-ONE

In Cumbria, 11 December dawned still and chilly. In the freezing air, noise seemed to carry much farther across the empty fields of the Lake District, and, from the hayloft, Kim heard the car. He stood on straw bales and, using his left eye only, peeked over the sill where it met the corner of the frame, exposing as little of his head as possible.

He watched the shiny maroon Jaguar pass the row of elms at the junction of the tracks, noticing how its suspension effortlessly handled the potholes. A Jag. Didn't detectives drive Jags? Confident he could be down the ladder noiselessly and into his bolt-hole in the old grain store in less than a minute he decided to wait and see.

Eddie Malloy had mixed feelings about Ludlow racecourse. It lay in a beautiful setting in south Shropshire against a background of rolling hills, within a twenty minute drive of home. But the track could be a tricky one to ride with the hurdle and 'chase courses having separate back straights. And four roads crossed the course. Although covered during racing by thick matting, they caught the odd horse by surprise and made him lose his action. The ground was often so firm, it regularly dealt out fractures to those unlucky enough to have a fall.

Eddie wondered as he walked through the gates this bright Monday morning whether he'd begun worrying more about the disadvantages of race riding. That was often the first sign of an inclination to retire. Every jump jockey's clock had only so many miles on it; you couldn't tell when yours was going to start packing up.

Maybe it was just a healthy jolt of self-preservation since he'd met Rebecca, an instinct to keep himself in shape for her and whatever lay ahead.

McCarthy waited by the front of the weighing room. The Security man wore the same long dark coat he'd been wearing to the races in the winter since Eddie had first met him. The man inside the coat hadn't changed much either, though well past forty now. A line extra on the face maybe, and a few grey hairs at the temple. But his hair was mostly black, and wavy, like that of the 1950s movie stars.

McCarthy stood six feet two and fought a constant battle with his weight, which Eddie guessed was around the seventeen stone mark.

'How goes it?' Eddie called with a smile while still ten strides away.

'Okay, I suppose.'

'Worries of the world, episode thirty-five.'

'Pardon?'

'You always look like you've got the worries of the world on your shoulders.'

'I have. Times ten.'

'Lots of people worse off than you, you know.'

McCarthy frowned, pushing himself away from the wall to walk with Eddie into the weighing room. He said, 'Lots better off, too. You can't trade on some worry index according to where you live, or what your circumstances are.'

'Or how much money you're worth, or what car you drive or blah, blah, blah.' Eddie said.

'Or how beautiful your girlfriend is.'

Eddie stopped and turned to look at him, but Mac was stone-faced and Eddie decided it had been a shot in the dark.

'What is it?' Mac asked, throwing his arms wide.

'Nothing. Where were we?'

'You were lecturing me on how lucky I am.'

Eddie slung his kitbag onto the slatted bench. 'Just get things into perspective, Mac, that's all I'm saying.'

McCarthy seemed wounded. Eddie clasped his arm and looked at him. 'I'm kidding, Mac. I'm winding you up. Come on, I'll fix you a cup of tea and we'll go for a walk in the sunshine.' Eddie preferred to be out of sight of others if he had to talk to McCarthy for any length of time. Mac was racing's equivalent of a cop. Eddie knew people talked about the fox running with the chickens.

But Mac had done him a few favours, pulled him out of some pretty deep holes. And Eddie had repaid in kind. They were not close friends, didn't socialize, but they trusted and respected each other. In Eddie's eyes, Mac was too bureaucratic and protective of his department, and he wouldn't be one to rely on when things got physical. But Eddie knew where he stood with him.

From McCarthy's viewpoint, Eddie was headstrong, took excessive risks and didn't give a damn for officialdom. But he knew he could depend on him. The security department had assessed Eddie as 'needy'. A seeker of approval. Skilfully set up, Eddie would do most things for you. Mac was never comfortable playing Eddie that way, but his boss always insisted he 'sweat the assets.' And his boss classed Eddie as an asset. Highly disposable, sometimes troublesome, but mostly useful.

Tea swilling darkly in white Styrofoam cups, they wandered outside and headed across the golf course laid out in the middle of the track. Eddie told McCarthy the Phil Grimond story leaving out Ben Turco. McCarthy didn't interrupt.

Standing at the edge of a deep sand bunker Eddie said, 'Before you start asking questions, Mac, there is someone else involved but I can't and won't tell you who it is. All I'll say is that the person won't do it again and that they are helping set up Grimond on Saturday.'

'So Grimond's the fall guy?'

'Grimond's an idiot. It's him that wants this on Saturday'

'But he's not in charge?'

'He's the one that won't let it lie. Making all sorts of threats.'

'But he's not the man behind everything?'

'He's the frontman, if you like.'

'So what good is he to us? The way I see it he's been getting in your man's hair and ...'

'Who said it was a man?'

'Is it a woman then?'

'I'm not saying, Mac. You make what assumptions you want.'

'My assumption is that whoever is masterminding the whole thing is using you.'

'You're entitled to your opinion. I don't think that's what's happening. And, by the way, that is rich coming from you.'

Mac opened his hands to make a point and spilled the remainder of the black tea into the white sand of the bunker. 'Eddie, what are you giving me here? You're giving me the bit player without the director? You're giving me the percussionist without the conductor! You're giving me the centre-half without the manager!'

'And you're giving me a headache, Mac! I'm giving you all I can. I'm not saying don't try and catch anyone else who's involved, I'm just saying you'll have to do it without me. I gave my word. Now, when I give you my word would you like to think I'm the type to keep it?'

'Of course! I know you are!'

'Well, stop bleating!'

Mac hung his head, kicked absently at some sand. 'Okay, but when we catch whoever's behind it, no pleas for mercy from you.'

'There won't be, don't worry.'

'Okay, what's the plan for Saturday?'

THIRTY-TWO

Through the thin opening in the hayloft doors, Kim watched the solicitor through eyes made watery by the cold wind. He'd liked Mr Ogilvie from first meeting him. Kim thought he would make a good uncle. He wondered why he'd come. Kim has been on the lookout for the Social Services people or the police, but not the solicitor.

Ogilvie walked up the path, pulling keys from his pocket. He opened the door to the house and went in.

Kim waited. From time to time he would faintly hear his name called.

After five minutes Kim saw him skirt the side of the house, still calling 'Kim!'. When he got behind the buildings up by the muckheap he was shouting something else but Kim couldn't make it out.

Eventually the solicitor came close to the barn, still calling out, but beginning to clear his throat more often. 'Kim! If you're here somewhere, if you can hear me, I want to help you! You don't have to go back to that place if you don't want to! We'll find a good alternative! You can choose it! I'll help you! I promise you that! Please just call me! I've left my card by the telephone in the house! Please call me and let me help the way your mum and dad wanted me to!'

Kim watched him turn full circle and look at the various buildings. As his eyes fixed on the barn Kim ducked down and instinctively held his breath. He stayed there until he heard the car door slam and the engine start, then slowly raised his head again, one eye following the Jag's elegant roll along the rutted track.

Kim pushed the hayloft doors fully open. On mornings like this he loved going riding, loved the feeling of being carried safe and dry through the icy mud and puddles. But Crystal wasn't here anymore.

There was always his bike, which had stood unused since the summer, its scarlet and lemon frame the only brightness among the tools, bins and boxes in the cluttered back porch.

After microwaved beans and a mug of tea Kim wheeled his bike out and set off down the drive, his tyres ploughing a deep mud furrow which had filled with seeping water by the time he reached the old oak at the junction.

He was gone for two hours, arriving home wet and muddy, face shining with health and fun, eyes sparkling. He switched on the radio in the kitchen, as his father used to do when he came in for his lunch. He drank a pint of icy water from the gushing tap then found a tin of fruit cocktail in the pantry. Then he remembered the creamed rice in his emergency stash in the loft in the barn.

Full of energy and tingling from the exercise, he climbed, smiling, to the loft and walked past the stacked hay bales to the old wooden box he kept his stuff in. As he opened it and grabbed the light blue tin, a voice behind him said, 'So you'll be Kim, then?'

His heart almost burst through his chest and the involuntary intake of breath sounded to Kim like the loudest sound he'd ever made. He dropped the tin as he turned and his eyes widened in shock as he saw a policeman sitting on a hay bale, elbows on his knees.

Kim lurched desperately at the ladder trying to escape. He'd never been in a bigger hurry but everything seemed to be happening in slow motion like on TV. Especially the fall. He tried to hold onto the top rungs as he lost his balance but something made him decide to let go completely. In the moments it took to plunge fifteen feet, he saw the brown stone floor coming at him, the old red tractor to his left, the lambing pens right in front, a rectangle of daylight through the main door, all spinning as he tumbled.

THIRTY-THREE

Eddie rode a winner at Leicester and was especially chuffed that Rebecca had hurried from the stands to the winner's enclosure to applaud him. He smiled at her and stooped to brush her hands with his fingertips as she reached up.

His other two rides were unplaced but she waited with words of comfort and encouragement, and Eddie felt the race was becoming secondary to the joy of Rebecca's beautiful smiling face as he rode back in.

After the last he hurried to the showers for his second shave that day, then took some good-natured ribbing as he produced a bottle of expensive aftershave from his bag. On his hook in the changing room, his valet, as requested, had placed a freshly laundered sky-blue shirt with double cuffs and brass collar-stiffeners. Beside this hung Eddie's best suit, navy blue, tailor-made. On the floor by the bench gleaming black shoes reflected the round bright lights above.

Eddie dressed quickly, checked himself as best he could in the big oval mirror and left to a chorus of wolf-whistles from his friends who were in various stages of undress.

Rebecca watched him walk smiling toward her and she put her hands out, stopping him, resting them softly on his shoulders. 'You look very handsome,' she said.

'And you look very beautiful.'

'Thank you.' Her earrings were pearl set in gold and her thick blonde hair held the same luxuriant sheen Eddie was beginning to love. He thought of the gathering of her hair, the weight, the luxury, the gloss of it, through his fingers, how it would feel to hold it suspended above her naked back before lowering it, arranging it on her skin ...

She took his arm and they walked toward the exit. They'd gone barely twenty strides when Eddie became aware of someone close behind him on his right. Frowning, he turned to see a plump, moustachioed face looking coldly at him. The man said, 'My name's Phil Grimond. I think you've heard about me. I've got something you'll want to see.'

'I doubt it,' Eddie said, still walking.

'Don't doubt it.'

'Go away.'

'Remember that odds-on chance you got stuffed on at Catterick last week?'

Eddie didn't acknowledge. He kept walking.

'I've got a picture of you taking a bribe from Tiny Delaware to stop it.'

THIRTY-FOUR

After a dinner, during which Eddie tried to make light of the six by four colour picture in his inside pocket, they drove to his flat. For the first time in a while Eddie felt he really needed the drink he held in his right hand. Rebecca had poured it, a big one over lots of ice, and Eddie was encouraged to see she'd taken an equally large one. She slipped off her shoes and folded her legs elegantly beneath her as she sat close to him on the feather cushions of the coffee coloured couch.

He'd already told her about Grimond, so didn't mind talking freely. He tried to be cool and conceal SiS deep worry.

Grimond couldn't have known that Eddie had set him up for Saturday, that McCarthy's men were on standby to raid the judge's box and 'discover' the software in use. The guy was doing what he'd promised Turco - 'dealing with Eddie'.

And Eddie knew Grimond had done just that.

How could he call McCarthy off now? Even if he could, it wouldn't be for long. The big man wouldn't wait unless Eddie put up a solid reason. If he allowed Grimond to be arrested, that picture would be the first thing the guy would produce. Eddie recalled the savage barracking from the Catterick punters and the looks of suspicion from the stewards at the Inquiry.

It set him thinking about the Catterick race again. Grimond must have stopped Keelhaul somehow. He'd heard nothing about the routine dope test on the horse, and assumed it showed negative.

But there were many in racing who believed that doping could be sophisticated enough to remain undetected. Keelhaul must have been got at, otherwise Grimond wouldn't have set up the bribing scene with Tiny?

He pulled the picture out again and cursed Tiny for conning him with that story about the autograph for the kid. He held the print under the light of the single lamp that burned on the table by the side of the couch, and Rebecca stretched across him to look down at it too. Sighing, he dropped the photo and leaned back, his head resting on the cushion.

He closed his eyes and breathed slowly through his nose. Then he felt her lips on his. Soft. Parted slightly. She rested them there. No movement. As though she were trying to still him, make him peaceful. Her body lay motionless. He could not even sense her breathing.

Then she did breathe. Her lower lip moved first between his lips, probing, prising them apart until his mouth opened. Then, shifting slightly sideways she pushed both her lips between his and her hands held his face gently but firmly. And she breathed into him, kissed him. And he began to relax, as though a drug had been injected. His pulse slowed. Peace washed over him. Later, when he lay awake thinking of it, he had no idea how much time passed, how long they'd stayed like that.

They'd gone from there to deep kissing then to gentle delicate finely edged kisses that could barely be felt and from there to passion and depth again. Then to the floor. To the rug. To the light and heat from the fire. From fully clothed to naked. Then bed.

And dreams for Eddie.

Dreams of a relationship that mattered for once in his life. At last in his lonely bloody God-damned trustless, fortressed life. Even though Grimond now loomed large and threatening. What could he do if he was finished as a jockey? How would he keep her? Somehow. Anyhow. Perhaps he'd take Turco up on his SiS scam and make that million he'd been promised. Lying in the darkness he laughed as he made plans for it with Rebecca and she laughed too when he told her of Turco's outrageous scheme.

And he rambled on into the night until he finally talked her to sleep. But Eddie stayed awake, wanting to watch her, to cherish the memory of what they'd done, of her being beside him.

Next morning, Thursday, after Rebecca left for London, Eddie rang Ben Turco and told him about Grimond.

'Shit!' Turco said.

'Any suggestions?' Eddie asked.

'My brain don't function too well this time of the morning. You riding today?'

'Leaving for Taunton within the hour.'

'Call you back.'

Eddie thought Turco hadn't grasped the importance of what he'd said. 'Ben, listen, this could finish me. Maybe we should cancel Saturday. I can put McCarthy off for another week or so.'

'What difference is that gonna make? If we don't go through with this on Saturday, Grimond becomes a bigger loose cannon. God knows where he'll go off next. And if you bow to this, it's like an admission of guilt. He'll be blackmailing you for something else then, asking you to fix races.'

Eddie hesitated. 'I know. You're right. I'll talk to McCarthy… get it out in the open.'

'Just hold off, Ed, gimme an hour or so before you do anything. I'll call you.'

THIRTY-FIVE

The reception on Ogilvie's mobile phone was poor and he felt embarrassed at having to shout into the mouthpiece. His voice boomed in the long corridor at Carlisle's Cumberland Infirmary. He'd have gone outside if the rain hadn't been sheeting down. The noise of it hammering on the windows made him shout even louder.

All he wanted his secretary to do was get Kim's file out and give him the telephone number of Mrs Malloy in Newmarket. As he waited he knew he'd have to find somewhere more private than this to make the next call from. But it would have to be made soon.

The solicitor had rarely moved from Kim's bedside in the past forty-eight hours. The boy remained comatose and the doctor could not say if or when he would come out of it. Ogilvie felt an enormous guilt. He'd become obsessed with being there when Kim opened his eyes, unable to bear the idea of Kim thinking he'd betrayed him by sending the police.

Good God, how had that fool of a policeman expected Kim to react? A child on the run taken utterly by surprise. How on earth could he fail to foresee the possible consequences? It was little consolation that the policeman had been suspended.

Doreen, Ogilvie's secretary, gave him the number and as he scribbled it inside a thin diary, Ogilvie vowed to travel south, determined to confront Kim's mother.

Driving to the races, Eddie finally got through to Peter McCarthy. 'Mac, I don't suppose you'll be at Taunton today?'

'Sandown.'

'Damn!'

'What's wrong?'

'I need to see you, Mac.'

'Something wrong?'

'Yes.'

'Surprise, surprise. What's up? Have we got a problem with your friend on Saturday?'

'Sort of.'

'Go on.'

'Mac, it's best not discussed on a mobile. Are you going home after Sandown?'

'Yes.'

'Can I call in on the way back from Taunton?' Mac cleared his throat. Eddie knew he was uncomfortable about inviting him to his house. 'Give me a call when you're half an hour away and we'll arrange to meet somewhere.'

'Fine. See you tonight.'

THIRTY-SIX

Eddie was luckless at Taunton, with four unplaced mounts. By the time he met Mac in the Chequers Hotel in Newbury, he felt the need of a large whiskey, but ninety more minutes of driving lay in front of him. So they sat in the lounge drinking mineral water. McCarthy carried the bowl of nuts from the bar to their table and plucked at them, dropping them into his mouth like some machine.

'Well, I see you're not a frequenter of bars,' Eddie said.

'Why?' asked Mac, chewing.

'You wouldn't catch the pros nibbling from those bowls. Think how many people go to the toilet, don't wash their hands, then come back and stick their fingers into the communal nuts and crisps.'

McCarthy scowled and pushed the bowl away from him. Eddie smiled. Mac said, 'I hadn't thought of that.'

'You will in future.'

The big man nodded then Eddie told him what happened with Grimond at Leicester.

Mac said, 'And have you got this photo?'

Eddie pulled the picture from his inside pocket and handed it over. Mac looked at it and tutted, shaking his head. 'This looks bad, Eddie.'

'Tell me something I don't know.'

Mac stared at it in silence, as if waiting for some strange metamorphosis. He waved the picture gently. 'This, my friend, whichever way you look at it, however things work out on Saturday, is going to cause you very big problems.'

Eddie knew that if Grimond chose to mount a campaign against him, then the picture, the defeat of Keelhaul, the allegations, would be investigated by Mac's people. McCarthy said he preferred not to discuss what his comments might be when asked to look at the case, and Eddie took this to be positive.

Different security officers handled the North East racecourses like Catterick, and Mac, although a senior officer, would have to buck the protocol to muscle in.

It occupied Eddie's mind all the way home, along with his other obsession, Rebecca. As soon as he got in, he called her and went over everything McCarthy had said. She made all the right comforting noises, offered reassurances and generally calmed him.

But he warned her of what lay ahead. 'Mac will only carry so much clout and he'll be up against some people, stewards, who simply don't like me. Nothing would please these guys more than to see me warned off again, see me out of racing for good.'

'But surely Tiny Delaware will confess he set you up?'

Eddie sighed into the mouthpiece. 'Something tells me that if this breaks Tiny will disappear until it's over.'

'Fine, then they can't try you without one of the chief witnesses.'

'Yeah, well who do you think will get the blame for Tiny suddenly not being around?'

'Then contact him now. Try tomorrow. Tell him you know what happened and that you need him to tell the truth when Grimond starts causing trouble.'

Eddie considered that. 'Maybe you're right. I'll try.'

'Where are you tomorrow?'

'Cheltenham.'

'Will Tiny be there?'

'He might be. We'll see. Anyway, enough of me moaning. It'll work itself out somehow.'

Rebecca said quietly, 'What if it doesn't work out, Eddie? What will you do?'

'It will. It will work out. Don't worry.' But his tone betrayed a lack of confidence.

After another pause Rebecca said, 'That offer, from your American friend, that SiS scam, would you really consider getting involved in that?'

Suddenly, the disadvantages of being in love but not really knowing the person you're in love with hit home.

Did she want him to do it?

If Turco's estimate of scooping millions was right, it would mean Eddie worries would be over. It would mean that come March, when Rebecca received her trust fund payment, he'd be on equal terms with her, at least for a while. To hell with the stewards and with racing and its petty jealousies. They could both live a bloody fine life from then on.

'It wouldn't matter if I did want to get involved because, if I was warned off, SiS wouldn't have me in the studio. The opportunity wouldn't be there anymore.'

'But would you do it if it was?'

She wasn't letting him off the hook.

'No, I wouldn't. I couldn't.'

'Good. I'm glad.'

Eddie smiled.

Exhausted, Campbell Ogilvie finally left the hospital at 11.15 p.m. to return to his family.

One of six critically ill patients in the small Intensive Care Unit, lit only by a softly glowing lamp beside each bed, Kim lay in the corner, hooked up to monitoring equipment, his body being fed intravenously. A few minutes after Ogilvie trudged wearily out of the room, Kim's eyelids flickered, then stilled.

Late that night, Phil Grimond was driving to his home, happy and excited by the next day's planned coup. And he'd got a real and unexpected charge from nailing Malloy. That feeling of control over another human being, an adult this time, carried much more pleasure than he'd imagined.

He looked at the clock on the dashboard: the first race was fifteen hours away. Come tomorrow, with normal luck, he'd be fifty grand richer. All he needed was a photo finish. He'd seen the runners in the evening paper: good competitive racing with every chance of a couple of close ones. And that bastard Malloy was out of the picture. Or rather, in the picture. Grimond smiled as he pulled into the long driveway of his house. Newly bought with a big mortgage, it was the main reason he couldn't let Turco throw sand over the campfire and roll the wagons off somewhere else.

Grimond still got a kick out of aiming his little remote control gadget at the garage and seeing the door swing up automatically. He'd mastered the art of doing it now without lowering the window.

Car lights off.

The garage was in darkness as Grimond locked the vehicle and pulled his jacket collar up against the cold night. Back on the driveway, he turned to aim his remote at the sensor when he was hit from behind, a pounding jab to the kidneys. He grunted and was struck again, heavily, knocking the air from him in a long gasp. He fell to his knees. Two men dragged him into the garage.

They held him down across the warm bonnet of the car. He gasped and coughed as his lungs tried to refill themselves. He was aware of nothing about the men but their strength. No sight, no smell, no touching of flesh. Then he felt fingers on his scalp, the heel of a hand on his face forcing his head against the bonnet, holding it hard there. He wanted to speak, to plead, but couldn't recover sufficiently.

He wasn't aware of what they used on him, didn't even sense it on his cheek at first. He would never be able to make up his mind whether it was searing hot or ice-crystal cold. He couldn't remember if he screamed. The doctors told him later that the shock of it probably brought on immediate unconsciousness. The police and ambulance crew thought it particularly morbid that the removed organs, eyes and tongue, were nowhere to be found.

THIRTY-SEVEN

Laura Gilpin cupped her hand around Eddie Malloy's shin, and legged him into the saddle of Samson's Curls in the paddock at Cheltenham. Turco had been trying to reach Eddie for the past ninety minutes to tell him Grimond had failed to check in. But Eddie had left his phone in the car.

When Laura wished him luck as she released the bridle, Eddie's mind was on bringing Samson's Curls as late as possible, while still managing to win by half a length or more, a distance he considered that Grimond wouldn't attempt to alter.

As her horse launched into a canter, Laura flinched, frowned and spun sideways to avoid the sandy kickback, then turned to watch the muscular rear end ripple. Her eyes moved upwards to Eddie's rear end in his white shiny breeches. She made a biting gesture and chuckled aloud, drawing some odd looks from spectators packed against the white rail.

McCarthy had briefed his colleagues who were going to 'assist' him when they burst in on Grimond in the judge's box. Eddie told him this race might well result in a close finish and that Grimond would have the DIM equipment primed. When McCarthy's men appeared at the meeting place by the weighing room as arranged, McCarthy wasn't there. He'd had the foresight, albeit late, to go to the racecourse office and check that Grimond would definitely be on duty.

In the stands, Laura, terrified but entranced, watched Eddie nurse the horse tenderly behind the leader, holding her breath for almost as long as Eddie had held the horse, then letting it out in a half scream, half cheer which pierced the crowd's roar as Eddie hit the front just before the line.

Red-faced, laughing with nerves and relief, Laura hurried to meet them. Back on the sandy canter lane, she barreled through the incoming horses and stable lads. Seeing her charging along with fierce purpose and obvious delight, made Eddie smile. By the time she got to them, she was crying. She kissed the horse's foam flecked muzzle as his velvety nostrils sucked and blew and his sides heaved.

She reached toward Eddie and he crouched and put an arm round her and kissed her forehead. 'Well done!' he said. She held onto him, still moving, crying and laughing until Eddie wasn't sure if she was holding him in the saddle or hauling him out of it.

'Who's the fat woman?' Rebecca asked him later.

Eddie smiled. 'That was Laura, the owner and trainer. Nice girl. I introduced you, didn't I?'

'You did but I was too busy trying to figure out why you were kissing and hugging her so much to remember her name!'

'I only kissed her twice!'

'Come on! When she got you in that head lock, I thought you'd suffocate in there.'

Eddie reddened.

'See,' Rebecca said, 'you're blushing!'

'Only because I felt embarrassed by it!'

Rebecca's phone rang, and Eddie was relieved at the distraction. Her teasing smile faded as she listened to the caller. Eddie walked away, wanting to give her privacy. He knew little of her life away from him and didn't want to smother her.

The call ended quickly. She slowly pushed the phone into her pocket as she walked toward Eddie. 'I'm sorry, I need to go. That was my sister. Mum is very ill.'

He reached for her but she stood straight-armed, brow creased, mind elsewhere. 'Can I help?'

She shook her head. 'No. No thanks. I'm sorry.' She looked at him.

He smiled, his hands on her shoulders. 'No need to apologize. You know where I am, if you need me.'

She kissed his cheek then turned and walked away. Eddie watched as she wandered through the crowd like a lost child. She seemed in no hurry to get to her mother's side and Eddie wondered what twists and knots had formed in the relationship between mother and daughter. 'Call me,' he shouted after her. She stopped and turned. 'Call me tonight. Let me know how your mother is.' She raised a hand and walked on. 'And drive safely. Try and stay below a hundred!' No turn. No smile. No wave.

THIRTY-EIGHT

The first voicemail Eddie picked up when he got in the car was from Ben Turco. He switched to hands-free, chose Ben's number, then joined the crawling queue of traffic heading through the deepening dusk for the exits.

'Eddie. Heard the news about Grimond?'

'No.'

'Somebody did a proper number on him last night outside his house.'

'Beat him up?'

'Cut him up. Gouged his eyes out and sliced off his tongue.'

'Jeez!'

'Sliced it off at the root after digging his eyes out of his head.'

Eddie hit the auto-lock on his doors. 'How did you find out?' he asked.

'I've got a link to the security cameras outside his house.'

'You saw it happening?'

'I watched the tape about twenty minutes after they got him. I always check through my stuff before bed.'

'Did you see who did it?'

'Two guys. Short, stocky. Hoods and dark clothes.'

'Fuck.'

'I couldn't see how bad they were hurting him. I got the detail afterwards from the police scanners.'

'Who was he tied in with? You thought somebody else was pushing him, didn't you?'

'Just a hunch. But if it was someone getting tips about the photo scams, they'd have known about the one planned for today, so why take out the guy who's about to make them money?'

'Maybe he didn't tell them. Maybe they found out late that he was planning a touch without them.'

'Could be. Anyway, it's the only warning I need. I'm gone. As I speak to you, I'm looking toward the door at where my trusty old suitcase is packed and tapping its tiny wheels impatiently, anxious to continue its career as a receptacle for the belongings of a living person; one with all facial features and limbs intact.'

'Where are you going?'

'The good old US of A. If this is to do with the DIM stuff I'd sooner take my chances in downtown New York. At least the muggers and panhandlers leave you your eyes and tongue.'

'How long will you be gone for?'

'Until, as they say, the heat dies down.'

'Any chance of the police tying you in with Grimond?'

'That depends on what Grimond kept lying around at home. I don't know if he made notes or kept a diary or something. Whatever, I'm in the frame from both sides. The perps might be looking for me and the cops too.'

'You think you can avoid extradition if it comes to it?'

'My homeland stretches to three point eight million square miles, my friend. I can fly a Cessna. And I can buy a Cessna. It will hold enough for a year's stay in a cabin beside an Alaskan lake.'

'Don't tell me any more, Ben.'

'Afraid they'll torture it out of you?'

'Something like that.'

'Why don't you come with me?'

'And make myself a fugitive for no reason? While you're cooking salmon by that Alaskan lake, I'll have other fish to fry.'

'That girl of yours?'

'Among other things.'

'Expect an invite for both of you for a week in Spain. From Walter.'

'Walter made it then? Permanent?'

'Yep. Majorca. Dream retirement. He says he'd never have got there if you hadn't been easy on him.'

'He's a nice man.'

'You're a nice man, according to him. No accounting for taste.'

119

'What about your other guy?'

'Magnus? I called him ten minutes ago. I'd guess as we speak that he's clicking the buy button on a flight to Malmo.'

'Whoever did Grimond in just boosted the emigration figures.'

'I'm hoping it was something to do with his sleazy hobby. Maybe we're running for nothing, but we're done here anyway. No point taking chances.'

'That's a first, from you.'

'Well good luck and au revoir and all that stuff. If ever you want to cream those bookies with that slice of genius I came up with - you know, with SiS - gimme a call.'

'Where?'

'I'll be in touch when I get there.'

'Ben, before you go, did Grimond have anything to do with the Chinese at any point? The Triads maybe?'

'Not to my knowledge. Why do you ask?'

'Just a thought.'

'Don't have too many of those. Bad for you. I'll see you around.'

'Good luck.'

'Same to you, Ed, same to you.'

Sitting in that race traffic in the early winter dark, Eddie watched the landing lights of a plane approaching Birmingham airport. The passengers could look down on the array of lights from thousands of vehicles trying to leave Cheltenham races. He was stuck in the middle of them, giving his mind time to dwell on what Grimond must have gone through.

He relived the vicious criminal onslaughts he'd survived since returning to riding. Skill, strength and courage carried him through, or so he'd believed until now. We all consider most other people to be less competent than we are; Eddie had particularly high regard for himself in these matters. But trapped in that ghostly fog of exhaust fumes, surrounded by a flickering random barrage of lights, he thought of Grimond and realized he himself had ridden a long streak of luck. A planned attack in cold blood by savage men might prove crippling or deadly, even to him.

How long does luck last?

A sliced-off tongue carried the taste of the Triads. Eddie believed they favoured such methods.

The hacked hand of Matt Nash came to his mind.

His phone glowed orange a second before it rang. His sister's name showed.

'Marie? Hello. Is everything all right?'

Her hesitation answered his question. 'Mum is okay, Eddie, but I need to see you.' She spoke quietly, in a sad monotone.

'What's wrong?'

'Nothing bad. Nothing...nothing medical. I'm not sick or anything. I've had some bad news. I don't want to tell you about it on the phone. I don't want to tell you about it at all, but I need to. Face to face.'

'And mother's not sick?'

'No sicker than she's been, no.'

'Look, I've got some gear with me. I can drive straight over once I'm out of this traffic jam. I can probably be there by eight.'

'Okay. Thanks.'

'You're not pregnant or something, are you?' Eddie asked lightly.

'No...no, I'm not pregnant.'

'I'm kidding, Marie. Cheer up. You're not sick. Whatever else it is, we can fix it.'

'I don't think so.'

'Listen. We'll fix it. I promise.'

'I'll see you when you get here.'

'Need anything? Want me to stop at the shops?'

'No. Thanks.'

'Okay. Keep your chin up.'

'Bye.'

Eddie watched her name disappear from his phone screen. His young sister. Three years his junior, sounding like an old woman, a sad old woman. What was wrong now? He recalled their last conversation and wondered if she'd finally had enough. And the guilt seeped into him once more. A wide-ranging scab he'd never been able to stop picking at.

He should have spent the past year trying to get to know Marie. When he'd first left home, he hadn't even said goodbye to the thirteen-year-old. When next he saw her, she was a woman, a stranger, at the funeral of their father, the mastermind of dysfunction.

Father had been the family puppeteer; mother, his collaborator - or one of the puppets - depending on his mood. There had been three children. Michael, the youngest, died when they were all still young and that's when the puppet strings on Eddie and Marie went haywire.

Eddie left as soon as he could. He was the one who'd suffered most at the hands of his father. He believed Marie would survive on her own, but he realized that even if he hadn't believed that, he would still have run.

When had Marie gone? When had she escaped? How old had she been? Eddie didn't even know that.

He had run out on her again a year ago. *Move in Marie, it makes sense, doesn't it? You can be with mother and it'll be an investment - the house, the stud. Perfect.*

Yes, perfect for Eddie Malloy.

He rubbed his eyes and sighed long and low. All he could do to make amends was fix this thing for her, whatever it turned out to be. Money, maybe. She wasn't in a relationship, as far as he knew...not sick. What remained?

Eddie realized he was in the wrong line for his turn now. He wanted to make a right for the road east to Newmarket. He clicked the indicator switch in the hope someone would let him in.

THIRTY-NINE

Marie opened the door of the house as he stepped out of the car. At five-nine, she stood almost as tall as Eddie. He watched her slim, unmoving outline against the light of the long hallway as he walked up the path.

He reached and hugged her. She did not unfold her arms.

She led him to the kitchen. 'I'll put the kettle on,' she said. 'Are you hungry?'

'I'm starving but I've got to do ten stone in the first at Fontwell tomorrow, so tea will be fine. Should I go and say a quick hello to mother?'

'She's asleep.'

'I'll look in on her. Quietly.' Eddie turned toward the door.

'She's in father's room.'

Eddie stopped. 'Since when?'

'Yesterday.'

'Why?'

'She said he would have wanted that.'

'She's probably right. He'd have wanted her to fill his deathbed and mourn the rest of her life away.'

'We're a mourning family, don't you know?' Marie said quietly, fixing the tea things, not looking at him.

'I'll be back in a minute,' Eddie said.

She lay on her side, lit faintly by the lamp on the small table behind her. The tight bun of white hair claimed most of that light, shining like some warning beacon. Her face was in shadow, her

123

body at rest under the pink blanket, so still that Eddie watched for the rise and fall of her breathing, involuntarily holding his own breath until he saw signs of hers.

He wondered what she might have been had she married someone else.

He wondered what she might have been had Michael not died.

What might they all have been then?

From her chair in the kitchen, Marie watched him come back in. All that lay between them was the corner of the big pine table and two blue mugs of tea.

Eddie sat facing her across that corner, close enough to touch, close enough to check for the tracks of her tears. He saw none.

He picked up the mug and sipped, watching her. She held his gaze with sorrowful eyes and said. 'I had a baby when I was fifteen.'

He watched her.

'He was adopted.'

'What's his name?'

'I called him Mark. His new parents called him Kim.'

'And he's at the age where he wants to meet you.'

'His father was killed in an accident two weeks ago. His mother died of cancer two years ago. There is no other family.'

Eddie searched her face for emotion. He saw only stress in her blue eyes, her clamped jaw, her bunched fists. 'Poor kid,' he said. 'How did you find out?'

'His father's solicitor contacted me.'

Eddie felt he should reach for her hand or move closer, but she seemed cold and hard. 'So what's to happen? Are you going to meet him? Kim, I mean?'

She stared at Eddie. 'He's in hospital in Carlisle. He's in a coma. He fell from the hayloft at the farm where he lived.'

He slid forward now, gripped her arm. 'Jeez, Marie, I'm sorry. No wonder you're shattered.' Eddie rose and pushed his chair in. 'Look, I'll take care of mother. I can call off my rides for the next few days. You get yourself up to Carlisle.'

'I can't.'

'Of course you can! Don't worry about anything here. I'll sort something out. Go and see your boy.'

Marie slammed the table with the flat of her hand and her face came to life. 'He's not my boy! He's a stranger. They pulled him out of me twelve years ago and took him away. I didn't get to touch him! I never saw his face!'

Eddie sat again and reached for the hand still flat on the table. She drew it away.

'You called him Mark. You gave him a name,' Eddie said quietly.

'I thought I'd have him for a few weeks, until they found somebody. I chose the name and hoped they'd let me christen him, at least. But they didn't. They said it was for the best and they were right. It was for the best. For me and for him.'

'Look, Marie, you're in shock. You'll-'

She jumped to her feet. 'Don't patronize me! I've had enough of that from that fucking solicitor! I'm not in shock. I'm close to halfway through my life and what do I have? Who have I got a relationship with? A sick old woman dying of self-pity, who couldn't protect her own children from their mental father. A brother I don't even know. A string of broken so-called romances so long I could tie a noose with them and hang myself. Don't you think my prospects are bad enough without taking in a twelve-year-old as well? Would *you* do it?'

'Yes, I'd do it. He's your son. He's your *son*! He's flesh and blood in this family, crippled as it is. Give him the chance we didn't get, for God's sake!'

She leaned across and stabbed at the air with her finger. '*You* give him a chance! He's your nephew, big flesh and blood man! What about her upstairs? She's your flesh and blood. What did you ever do for her?'

'What could I have done, Marie? Tell me that.'

'You could have done your share. You could have done your bloody share! I got saddled with it. Your share as well as mine.'

He held her wild gaze...'I'm sorry,' he said softly, and lowered his head. Marie looked down at him, waiting.

Eddie stood, feeling for his car keys. 'Which hospital in Carlisle?'

She sank into her seat and rubbed her face, her dark hair falling forward, hiding all but her hands. 'Cumberland Infirmary,' she said quietly.

He put a hand on her shoulder. 'I'll call you.'

She nodded, face still covered.

'I'll fix it, Marie.'

She didn't respond and wouldn't look at him.

He left.

She sat in the silence that had closed in on her this past year, a silence she'd become so intimate with that she sensed the fractures in it from the shouting, and she wondered if it would come back together again as air does after lightning. No thunder though. Please.

She looked at the ceiling, knowing her mother would have heard the ranting, the rise and fall of the family argument. And Marie wondered if her mother felt as she had done, lying upstairs, all those years ago, a baby in her belly and fear in her heart. And hopelessness in knowing that father would shout mother down, as always.

This time, *this* time… the woman won.

Eddie drove away quickly, trying to show a sense of purpose, in case Marie was watching. He didn't see his mother's figure at the upper window, framed in the angle of the parted curtain, looking on from the edge.

Half a mile down the dark road, he pulled over and switched off the engine. It was after nine. Carlisle was four hours north. He was unshaven and felt dirty. Dirty and guilty and angry at being guilty; resentful of Marie for making him feel this way. Angry with her for abandoning her son. Twelve. Around the same age as Eddie had been when his father cast him into the emotional wilderness.

Twelve. Orphaned. In a coma. And she wants to abandon him? A Malloy? Not this time. Not for this generation. Not for this child.

He started the car.

FORTY

Eddie sped through the night. The M6 motorway carried him north across the Lake District and, thirty miles from Carlisle, a border city, the clouds suddenly ended. Eddie's car rolled alone on the road under a full moon and a skyful of stars. To the west, a rank of dark mountains on the horizon; to the east, meadow and moor. Ahead, an empty ribbon of road. No artificial light but that from his front beams. He felt like the last man on earth.

He was special.

Again.

He switched off his headlights and relied, for a while, on the moon, his instincts, and the shot of adrenaline that came from his vision of traveling across a dark deserted planet at a hundred miles an hour.

The night nurse at reception offered to lead him all the way to Kim's ward.

'Abandoning your post?' Eddie said, smiling.

'All quiet on the western front,' she said. 'It will take me two minutes and save you ten minutes wandering.'

On the walk, she told him that Mister Ogilvie, the solicitor had been with Kim all evening, not leaving until late.

'He's a good man,' Eddie said, suggesting he knew him, concerned in case the nurse would ask for some ID, some proof he was Kim's uncle. He resisted too asking how the boy was, or what the specialists were saying.

The nurse introduced Eddie to the man in charge of ICU, nurse Adebayor. They shook hands and Eddie followed him to Kim's bedside. The nurse eased a chair out for him and smiled.

'Is your phone switched off?'

'It's in the car,' Eddie said, making a mental note to contact Marie and tell her he'd arrived.

The nurse nodded and left him.

Eddie stood looking at the boy, seeing a strong resemblance to himself at that age: dark, almost black hair, curly and thick, and that well-defined jawline and cheekbones, his skin coloured by the sun, but the Celtic genes resisting a tan.

Eddie looked at Kim's feet and tried to judge his height, already sizing him for a riding career.

Eddie would bet Kim's eyes were blue.

A patient coughed, and Eddie became aware that the ward held five others. He looked around, taking in the sounds more than the sights…pumps working, soft beeps, breathing, the ticking clock on the wall above: 1.30.

He turned back to his nephew. The visual register had been ticked. A Malloy. No doubt. Lying there, unable to communicate, his sister's son. For the first time, Eddie wondered who the father was, where he was?

No matter.

The boy needed family now. Eddie watched Kim's strong steady breathing. A cannula on the back of his right hand channeled liquid into his body.

Eddie felt with certainty that the boy would come through this. He was as sure of that as he had been less than an hour ago, hurtling through the night, of his own special place in the world.

Belief.

Faith.

Not in religion or doctors; faith in judging his intuition, his instincts.

'All will be well,' he said quietly to Kim. Eddie smiled. 'All will be well.' And he took his jacket off and settled in the chair by the side of his sister's son.

An hour later, Eddie remembered he had not contacted Marie. He told the nurse he'd be back soon and hurried to the car. Eddie decided to send a text. Marie might be asleep. And what would he have said to her, anyway?

He noticed two missed calls from Matt Nash. And a voicemail. He played it: Matt sounding drunk: "Eddie. Sorry to call so late, mate. I think I just saw Rebecca being hustled into that club, that casino, by the Chinese. You know, the one they took me to. Can't be sure, but thought I'd be better safe than sorry. Anyway, call me in the morning."

FORTY-ONE

Eddie sat in the dark cold car, staring at the phone screen.

What to do?

He slumped. His head went back on the padded rest and he looked through the sunroof. The stars shone as brightly as on the road, hours ago, but that special feeling had gone, carried off by weariness.

He checked his watch: almost twenty four hours without sleep. His body might have withstood another long drive through the night, but his mind would not. Beset by tiredness and waves of emotion and commitments to Marie and to Kim…well, whatever trouble Rebecca was in, if it had been her Matt saw, there was nothing Eddie could do about it. Not now.

He tried Matt's number. It went to voicemail. He rang Rebecca: voicemail.

She'd gone with her mother, hadn't she? To Norfolk. Far from London. Safe from the Chinese. Matt must have made a mistake. A blonde glanced on a drunken night out. Being "hustled". What did that mean?

Eddie sighed and threw aside his phone and rubbed his face. He needed to stay with Kim. If it turned out that something *had* happened to Rebecca, well, what could he have done? Three hundred miles away. Hours and hours. Whatever they planned to do to her would have been done anyway, by now.

He cursed. He felt his conscience being smug with him and was about to argue with it, aloud. He tried to think that through and said, 'I'm going mad.'

He switched the phone off and put it in his pocket and he returned to the warm ward, to his nephew, to a comfortable chair where sleep overcame him.

When the nurse shook him gently awake and Eddie saw her face, he thought he'd been injured in a fall. 'What happened?' He asked, then realized he was in a chair.

'You fell asleep beside your nephew. Some night watchman you are,' said the nurse, a woman of middle age whose natural kindness had blossomed in her long career. 'Would you like some coffee? No Danish pastries, I'm afraid, but I could scratch up a chocolate biscuit from somewhere, if you want?'

'No. No, thanks. Coffee would be fine. Black. No sugar. Thank you.' He straightened and stretched and looked at Kim, and the last twenty four hours came rushing at him, leaving him stunned. He checked his watch, felt for his phone. One of his shoes lay on its side, under the bed. Elbows on knees, he stared at the shoe.

A cardboard beaker of coffee loomed in his sight line and a voice said, 'Inhale deeply. That'll wake you up.'

He took it and smiled up at the nurse. 'Thanks.' He reached in his pocket. 'What do I owe you?'

'It's on the house. A sympathy drink. It's a long time since I saw a man look so bedraggled this early in the morning.'

Eddie smiled and sipped. 'I probably smell too.'

'I'll take your word for it.'

Eddie stood up and offered his hand. 'My name's Malloy. I'm Kim's uncle.'

The nurse shook his hand. 'So I hear. It's good to see family with him. I'm nurse Kelleway.' Eddie could see the tiny tangled root-system of veins on her cheeks that caused the bright bloom, and the whites of her hooded eyes were dull with broken vessels. Her jawbone rested in the fat of her neck, and Eddie thought she looked ill. But her smile was kindly and Eddie asked if she was by any chance related to the Kelleways from Newmarket.

'Not so far as I know, but given the shenanigans in my family, I'd rule nothing out.'

Eddie laughed. 'I'm grateful for the coffee.' He raised the cup in a toast. 'Have you a couple of minutes to tell me about Kim's injury?'

'Surely. Surely. Just let me get his notes.'

She sat with Eddie and told him of the tests they'd done and that Kim's consultant wouldn't see him again until tomorrow, given this was Sunday.

'I know a brilliant Neurosurgeon, Kenneth Trevorrow,' Eddie said. 'Have you heard of him?'

'I've met him a few times. He specialises in your business, doesn't he, sports injuries?'

'He does. Do you think Kim's consultant would object to me asking Ken to take a look at him?'

'Mister Palmer will be delighted, I should think. He's a friend of Mister Trevorrow.'

'That's good. I'll call him this morning. Will it be okay for me to stay here with Kim until he comes round?'

'I'm sure it will. It's encouraged with coma patients.'

'I'll try not to be a nuisance.'

She smiled and patted his hand. 'We keep special medicine for nuisances. Knocks 'em out flat.' She stood, surprising Eddie with the grace of her movement as she rose from the low chair.

'You can probably expect to see some of your mates in here later,' she said.

Eddie looked baffled.

'Racing at Carlisle today, isn't there? Rare that they all head home without a bruise.'

'Of course. I forgot. I'm supposed to be at Fontwell, the other end of the country.' He nodded toward Kim. 'Got a good excuse for calling off, eh?'

'None better, Mister Malloy. None better. You'll get the best phone reception out in the car park.'

'Thanks. I'll let you get on.'

'I'll be around until two. Just shout if you need anything.'

'I will. You've been so kind. Everyone here has been so helpful.'

'Our friends in the north.'

'Indeed. By the way, how did you know I'm a jockey?'

'I know a lot about you.'

Eddie waited, half-smiling.

'You've got a scar about two inches long on your scrotum.'

Eddie blushed until his cheeks were the shade of hers. 'I got kicked at Hexham, years ago. The horse's plate was hanging off and the nail ripped me.'

'I remember it well. I did the needlework. I was very pernickety about that job. Like stitching lace. I hope you've had no complaints since?'

He laughed. 'None. None at all. Should I tip you?'

'The pleasure was all in the work Mister Malloy.'

He raised the cup once more in a final toast.

Eddie finished his coffee and went to the bathroom. 'You look like shit,' He said to his reflection, confronting him from the waist up, across the many creases off his blue shirt to the heavy beard shadow and red eyes.

FORTY-TWO

Dawn was still more than an hour away, and a wind that had risen in the arctic and crossed the border, blasted the last remnants of sleep from him as he hurried through the car park.

He called Pat Kinsella and apologized to the trainer for having to cry off his Fontwell ride.

He phoned Matt Nash.

'Eddie. I saw your missed call. Didn't want to ring you back too early on a Sunday. Sorry.'

'You heard from Rebecca? What happened?'

'I don't know. No, I haven't heard from her. We were in town last night, after Cheltenham. Monty flew us down, took us out. Billy big balls, you know what he's like.'

'You went to that casino?'

'No! Are you kidding? I'm shitting myself passing it in Monty's limo, and that's got bulletproof windows. I just thought I saw her, between two men, hustling her up the steps. But I'm not sure now. I'd had a few. Maybe I just saw what I expected to see around there after what happened.'

'Did you see her face?'

'No. Her hair. And her walk, you know. But it was dark. Look, I'm sorry. I just wish she'd call.'

'She's in Norfolk. Her mother's ill. She told me she probably wouldn't get a signal down there.'

'Why didn't you say? Fuck! That's a relief!'

Eddie stopped himself from saying Matt sounded glad his investor and her trust fund were safe, rather than his friend, Rebecca.

'Did she say when she's due back?' Matt asked.

'Her mother took ill suddenly. She was pretty upset.'

'If she calls you, will you ask her to ring me?'

'I will. Likewise, eh?'

'Sure. You at Fontwell today?'

'I can't make it. Some family stuff came up.'

'Nothing too bad, I hope, mate?'

'Me too. Don't mention it to anyone, Matt, okay?'

'Sure. Of course. Let me know if there's anything I can do.'

'Just call me if you hear from Rebecca before I do.'

'I will.'

Eddie searched for Laura Gilpin's number. He told her he couldn't ride for her at Doncaster on Tuesday, as planned. She didn't probe, but Eddie found himself staying on the phone longer than he'd intended. She was easy to talk to. He felt comfortable with her, and ended up telling her about Kim.

When he returned to the ward, a man was sitting by Kim's bedside.

FORTY-THREE

Campbell Ogilvie smiled and introduced himself and shook Eddie's hand. 'Your sister told you, then?'

'Last night. As you can see by the state of me. I look worse than most of the patients.' Eddie rubbed his stubbled jaw as he reached for a chair and pulled it closer to the bed. 'Did Marie tell you she was going to, well...' Eddie searched for words that would not fall too harshly on his sister, '...get me involved?'

The solicitor shifted in his seat. 'In a way, she did.'

Eddie watched him, read him. 'You pushed her into it, didn't you?'

'Very unprofessional of me, I'm afraid. When I realized she was from the racing family Malloy, I did a final bit of checking before going to see her.'

'Did you threaten to tell me about Kim if she didn't?'

'I wouldn't put it quite so strongly as that.'

'And you'd read about my childhood so you knew I wouldn't stand for it?'

'Kim has no one else. I'd known him only a couple of weeks, but I would have adopted him myself if it were possible. How much do you know about him?'

'That he's my nephew and he fell from a hayloft.'

Ogilvie got up. 'Let me get us some coffee and I'll tell you the rest.'

Laura Gilpin parked and strode through the darkness and the icy rain, head up, smiling, no umbrella.

They wouldn't let her into the ICU to surprise Eddie.

She waited in the corridor.

Eddie smiled when he came out and saw who 'the visitor' was. 'You look worse than me. I guess it's raining.'

'I think drowned and rat are the words you're searching for. At least I don't look like a vagrant.'

He nodded toward the big brown bag hanging from her shoulder. 'Bag lady,' he said.

'We're well matched then.'

'A pair of tramps,' Eddie said, 'in the nicest possible meaning of the word. For you, at least.'

She smiled. 'Do you want a wet, cold hug?'

'You'd be useless at sales, Laura.'

They hugged and he kissed her cheek. 'You're quite warm, actually.'

'There's much to be said for good insulation, Mister Malloy.'

'Now you do sound like a sales lady.'

Eddie persuaded the nurse to let them both in to sit with Kim. 'She'll be going soon,' he said.

Laura leaned close to him as they followed the nurse. '*You'll* be going soon, mister. I came here to give you a break.'

When Laura saw Kim she seemed transfixed. She stood at the foot of his bed and bent forward, resting her hands on the metal frame, and she stared unblinking, for what seemed, to Eddie, a long time.

He watched her face. The light in the unit was low, as though a way had been found to share the output from just two bulbs throughout a dormitory. But the glow from the bank of monitoring panels around Kim seemed to highlight Laura's face. Eddie was struck by the intensity in her eyes and by a prettiness he hadn't seen before in her.

'He's going to do something big in life, Eddie,' she said. 'I don't mean make a million or be a big star or something, he's going to do something for people, for the world.'

'When I first saw him, I got the feeling right away that he was going to be okay.'

'He'll be more than okay, I promise you. Jeez, he looks so much like you. Have you got any pictures of yourself at that age?'

'I don't think I have.'

Laura took off her coat and sat down. She rolled up the sleeves of her green jumper, and Eddie felt a strange comfort in that gesture.

'Why are you looking at me like that?' Laura asked.

'Like what?'

'Like something nobody has ever seen before but believes they just might find amusing some day?'

'I didn't know I was capable of such subtlety.'

She smiled very gradually and warmly and softly, and he did too.

'Get yourself home Eddie Malloy and get cleaned up. And sleep in your bed for a few hours before you come back. I'll stay with Kim.'

'You have a business to run, Miss Gilpin.'

'Business, schmusiness. Go.'

He went to her and they hugged, holding on this time, in silence. They broke slowly, their gaze holding as they did, so that it felt that they hadn't broken at all, but joined.

The warmth of feeling Laura left him with prevented Eddie from phoning his sister and ranting at her as he traveled south. Yesterday he would have done exactly that; called her, nailed her, blamed her.

But something had changed. He didn't know what. Maybe tiredness. Maybe Kim. It couldn't be Laura. That was too hard to understand. Eddie had never had a friend. He knew many people, and liked quite a few of them. But he'd never considered any a friend, not in the way he'd heard others talk of friends.

He suspected now he might have found one in Laura. It couldn't be love. He felt nothing sexual for her. But as the miles steadily rolled by on the motorway, he decided that if this was what true friendship brought, he'd definitely have traded it for many of his sexual relationships. Maybe even all of them.

How strange…How strange.

FORTY-FOUR

Before going up to his flat, Eddie went into the big house and told Charles Tunney what had happened.

'I need to stay with him, Charles. I don't know when I'll be riding again. I'm sorry.'

The trainer held up a hand to hush him. 'No need to apologize, Eddie, for God's sake! Of course you must stay with him. Do you want me to let Broga know?'

'He won't mind, will he?'

'He'll be his usual laid back self. Expect him to offer to pay for the best of care for Kim.'

'I'm going to ask Ken Trevorrow to look at him. He'll do it for nothing.'

'Well you know Broga, he's going to want to help somehow.'

Eddie looked at the trainer. 'This will sound daft, Charles, but I think I'm beginning to grasp the true meaning of friendship.'

Charles shrugged and smiled. 'Want a drink?'

'No thanks. A shower? Yes. A shave? Definitely. But I'll pass on the drink, for now at least.'

He slept first. Set his alarm to ring after an hour, and stretched out under the covers, feeling his weariness dismantle in body sections, then wanting to stay awake just to hold softly onto that aura of semi-conscious peace, as exhaustion surrendered to the comfort and security of bed.

As 9pm closed in, Eddie hurried to finish his sandwich and tea, keen to be back on the road. He picked up his bag, enough inside to do him for a week. He looked in the mirror. His face glowed. His hair was still damp. He sniffed and screwed up his nose: too much deodorant, made worse by a rare splash of some aftershave he'd found after an obstinate search.

He hurried downstairs and out into the wind, which chilled his moist scalp and rattled the bare branches along the avenue of beeches, drowning the engine noise of the car whose headlights Eddie saw coming down the road through the trees.

He put his bag in the back and waited. An Audi, shiny and new looking in the wide flare of the security lights at the side of the building.

Two cops got out. Eddie had seen enough policemen in his time to recognize one before he reached for his warrant card. Eddie did a double take on them; for a few seconds he thought they were twins. But as they came closer he saw one looked maybe ten years older and that he dyed his hair that reddish brown colour to keep it looking the same as his mate's.

They were five nine, had moustaches, brown eyes, the older's slightly more hooded, more wrinkled. They wore dark suits, white shirts, plain narrow ties, black shiny shoes. Close up, the older one's skin seemed bad, pitted. He said, 'Wild night.'

'It is.' Eddie said.

'We are cops.'

Eddie smiled.

'We are tired cops who should have gone off duty before sunset.'

Eddie wondered what was coming next.

'We are cops who've managed to get lost three times looking for this place, courtesy of me being an idiot who can't read a map.'

Eddie looked at the other one who was smiling now, but not looking at his partner.

'You are very honest cops.' Eddie said.

'We are. We are.' He held out his hand. 'I'm Blackstock. He's Reid, both of us saddled with lifelong careers in Her Majesty's force.'

Eddie shook hands. 'I'm Malloy, saddled with a lifelong career as third rate jockey and very unlucky person in general.'

'Hallelujah! The first break we've had all day, for you are the very person we have come to interrogate.'

'Do you anticipate this interrogation taking long?'

Blackstock knitted his brows and put a comic hand to his chin, rubbing it. 'That depends on so many things. It's a tough one, Mister Malloy. No denying it.'

'I need to be in Carlisle by midnight. My nephew is in hospital there. I'm next on watch.'

Blackstock put a hand on Eddie's shoulder. 'We'll be as quick as we can. Do you want to sit in the car?'

'Come upstairs. I'll make coffee.'

The cops sat on the sofa. Eddie stood by the fire. Reid, the younger one, took over the talking.

'We'd like to talk to you about Philip Grimond.'

Eddie nodded and resisted sipping his coffee in case they read it as a nervous gesture.

'You knew him?' Reid asked

'Met him once.'

'Recently?'

'Last week.'

'Where?'

Eddie said, 'Let me try and save you a long question and answer session.' He told them what Grimond had done and why.

They listened without interrupting, then Reid said, 'So you think he set you up?'

'Uhuh.'

'Why?'

'I told you, he was running a scam with photo finishes, I knew what he was doing and was trying to get him stopped.'

'But he wanted to carry on so he set you up and threatened you?'

'Correct.'

'What did you tell him?'

'Nothing. I wasn't afraid of him, of the threat. I carried on with my side of things.'

'Which were what?'

'Informing Jockey Club Security. Have a word with Peter McCarthy there.'

Reid noted the name. 'Can you tell me where you were the night Grimond was attacked?'

'Which night was he attacked?'

'Friday.'

'I rode at Taunton on Friday, then met Peter McCarthy in a hotel in Newbury. Then drove home. Here.'

'What time did you get in?'

Eddie shrugged. 'I don't know, maybe nine, nine fifteen. I had a long phone call then with a friend. That should show up on phone records, by way of an alibi.'

'Was that a regular meeting with Mister McCarthy?'

'What do you mean?'

'A weekly, or monthly social meeting, a friendly catch up?'

'No. It wasn't. I wanted to tell him about Grimond and how he'd set me up, as I mentioned a minute ago.'

'What did Mister McCarthy say?'

'He said it was something he'd need to look into.' Eddie was sure they'd already spoken to Mac.

'Were you angry?'

'Pissed off and mad at myself for being so stupid with Tiny, but angry's probably the wrong word.'

Reid looked at his partner, who'd been writing quickly on a pad. He turned back to Eddie. 'There was blood at the scene which didn't come from Mister Grimond. Would you be willing to have a sample of DNA taken?'

'Sure.'

Eddie gave them his contact details. He read through Blackstock's notes and signed them off as his statement, then went downstairs with them and out to the car.

They shook hands. 'If you're in a huge hurry to get to Carlisle, I could probably call in a favour and get you an escort,' Blackstock said.

'Thanks. The roads should be quiet all the way at this time. I might call you in the morning and ask you to trade the escort for a torn up speeding ticket.'

The cops smiled.

FORTY-FIVE

The midnight radio news ended as Eddie pulled on the handbrake in the hospital car park.

Kim lay exactly as he'd left him. Laura was asleep, her head resting on her forearms, sandy hair spread out covering her face. He eased himself onto the chair beside her and reached for Kim's hand. Only the skin warmth told him the boy wasn't dead; the hand itself felt lifeless.

He looked again at Laura, her breathing deep and even, sucking a few strands of hair with each breath. Tenderly, Eddie reached to draw the hair from her face. She looked contented, the lightest sheen of sweat on her brow. He smiled and stroked her hair feeling a sudden intense gratitude and affection.

Kim's nurse came in at one o'clock and checked the instruments Kim was connected to and whispered that she'd call back soon to turn him. Laura stirred, waking woozily. She moved her head, resolved to settle again and sleep some more. She half opened her eyes and saw Eddie smiling.

She sat up slowly and leant toward him, putting her arms around him, nestling her head into his chest. Eddie smiled and held her, his smile growing wider at her dazed sleepiness. Then her right arm slid down to rest between the chair and the base of his spine and her left arm slipped softly across his lap.

And he fell asleep too.

An hour later they woke still semi-entwined and even in the warmth of their closeness and the heat of the ward, Eddie noticed

Laura's deep blush as she realized this was all real. She straightened and edged away, fixing her hair and her wrinkled blue dress.

Eddie smiled. 'Good morning.'

'Good morning. Eh, when did you get back?'

'Just after midnight. You were asleep.'

'I'm sorry. I meant to wait up.' She rubbed her grey-blue eyes like a sleepy child. 'What time is it now?'

'Very late. Time you were home.'

She sighed and stretched. Eddie said, 'I'll get us some coffee. You hungry?'

'For chocolate.'

'Chocolate it is.'

Over the hot drinks, Eddie tried to persuade Laura to go home. They'd adapted to talking softly in the ward, but when a nurse raised a finger and looked at them, Eddie led Laura into the corridor.

Laura won the argument. She was staying. Her staff could run the yard for a day or two. Come morning, she'd watch over Kim while Eddie organised a hotel for himself and sorted out his riding schedule and spoke to Kenneth Trevorrow.

At 9am, Eddie called Trevorrow. The surgeon was in New Zealand, away for three weeks. Eddie cursed. He drew a blank too with Rebecca, and didn't bother leaving a voicemail. He decided that if she'd been hurt by the Chinese, he would have heard about it by now.

Next he brought up his sister's number. He looked at her name on the screen and decided he couldn't stomach a family argument. Anyway, she needed confronting face to face. Without the threat from Campbell Ogilvie, Eddie would never have known at all. Kim would be lying in there alone. What class of heart did you own to do that to your son?

Kim's consultant, Malcolm Palmer, visited at noon. Eddie introduced himself. Palmer told him Kim's scan showed bruising to the cerebrum, which could worsen. Kim "showed no response to external stimuli", the classic symptom of the comatose patient. There was no way of knowing how long this would continue: he might wake tomorrow or in two weeks.

He and Laura returned to their vigil.

Mid-afternoon, Eddie went outside to walk a mile, to think, to try and get some sense of the real world back. After ten minutes heading north under darkening skies, he could smell water. On the edge of a wood, he cut through the trees, glad to be breathing cold air. His phone vibrated: voicemail from Rebecca. He stopped under an oak and dialled her number.

'Eddie! God, it feels like weeks since we spoke. Are you okay?'

'Are you? Matt called me in a panic yesterday saying he thought he saw you in London being hustled into that casino we found him in.'

'You're kidding! This is the first time I've been far enough away from that bloody cottage to get a phone signal. I've got a dozen voicemails to listen to. I wanted to call you before starting on them. What's Matt on about?'

'Oh, his heart's in the right place, I suppose. He'd had a few too many, probably. How's your mother?'

Rebecca said her mother was much better and that she hoped to return soon to London. He told her about Kim. She said she'd go straight to the Dorchester and pack a bag and fly up. Eddie persuaded her it was pointless to do that. He didn't mention Laura.

Back in the ward, Laura watched him approach. She smiled. 'You look all windswept and interesting,' she said.

'I'll admit to the first one.'

He sat beside her. 'I can actually smell the wind in your hair, you know,' Laura said.

He smiled. 'Even through a couple of layers of aftershave from last night?'

'Is that what it was? I thought one of these Cumbrian farmers mistook you for a lost sheep and hauled you through the dip.'

'Eh, I think you mean a ram, Miss Gilpin.'

'You're a big hit for yourself, Mister Malloy.'

'I'm kidding.'

'I know you're kidding.'

'Your turn for a break. Take a walk on the wild side.'

She got up and reached for her bag. 'I might just do that.'

As Eddie watched her go, he decided he'd have to buy her a Christmas present. And Rebecca too.

Christmas was eight days away. He looked at Kim. What Christmas gift do you get for a twelve-year-old boy in a coma? His mother?

Should Eddie go to Newmarket and have a crack at persuading Marie to see the boy? Even if it were only while he lay unconscious? Like peeking at him through a one-way mirror. Damn it, why should he let her off with just that?

Once Kim recovered, he'd take him down there and make Marie face him; make his mother face him.

Christmas. Boxing day. His big ride on Prince Simba in the King George. Again he looked at the unconscious boy. That would be a great present - Kim seeing his uncle win the King George.

FORTY-SIX

Despite their agreed watch schedule, tiredness overcame them and below the wall clock showing 5am on 18 December, they slept, heads resting on the bed on crossed forearms, elbows touching, breathing in the same rhythm.

All Kim saw when he woke were the mops of hair. His muscles ached and his skin felt raw in places. He turned, trying to ease the soreness in his back, then felt the pull of the needle in his hand as the long tube swung, moving the bag it fed from.

Kim closed his eyes again.

Then opened them. Things still made no sense. If he was alive he reckoned he must be in a hospital. Chin on his chest he raised his head; what was wrong with these others in the beds around him? Why was the ward so small and poorly lit? Who were these people asleep on his bed?

Where was Dad?

Dead.

It came to him now with the hammer blow of that single word in his brain. A blow that seemed to clear the jam in his memory and everything started flowing. Almost everything. Things came to a halt during the bike ride, the last thing he could remember. Riding his bike along the road. Spraying mud and water. Laughing. Passing sheep as he sped down the hill. Breathing hard and pedalling harder on the way home. He couldn't remember reaching the farm. Must have fallen off his bike and hit his head.

And who were these two? Had they found him? Perhaps they'd come from the children's home to take him back as soon as he woke up. Probably. Best then if he slipped away before they woke.

But what about his clothes, and where would he go? Why send two people from the home to wait for him? From the little he could see of them he recognized neither from Mr Young's children's home. Perhaps they'd come from a tougher place. Maybe it was like those war films: when you escaped they put you into an escape-proof one next.

One of them moved.

Kim closed his eyes. A minute passed. He opened his right eyelid a millimetre; a woman, still asleep. He could see her face now, round and pleasant but red-cheeked and warm looking. He opened both eyes then closed them immediately as the door opened. He heard someone come in, felt movement as the couple at his bed stirred, heard a whispered 'Good morning.'

Then the woman on the bed spoke quietly. 'Sleepyhead.'

'Mmmm?' Kim heard him stretch and yawn.

She said, 'You fell asleep on watch. The Indians could have caught us and tied us to a totem pole or boiled us alive or something.'

'I feel like they already have. It's warm in here.'

'Want some tea?'

'I'll get it. Have to go to the loo anyway.'

'Don't forget to wash your hands.'

He heard the man leaving then listened to the woman sigh and yawn. In a few minutes, the man returned. As he sat down again Kim could smell coffee; as strong a smell of coffee as he'd ever experienced and he would have loved some. She said, 'Eddie, I think Kim's hand moved through the night.'

'Which one?'

'The right one.'

The hand, which suddenly took his, caught Kim by surprise and he tensed slightly. The man said, 'I felt something then!'

Kim didn't know what to do and inadvertently found himself holding his breath. Her hand stroked his forehead now and he knew he wouldn't be able to play dead much longer. She touched his hair. 'I think you may well have your nephew home by Christmas.'

He opened his eyes.

Eddie stared at him. Kim held his breath. Eddie saw his nephew's deep blue eyes, and Kim thought he could be looking at a mirror from the future so closely did this man resemble him. This man.

His uncle.

FORTY-SEVEN

Eddie and Laura were quickly expelled from the ward while tests were carried out on Kim. They ate breakfast in the cafe.

'You look like you got stunned with a cattle prod,' Laura said.

Eddie chewed toast and smiled and raised his hands in a "What can I say" gesture.

'Have you decided how much you're going to tell him?'

'About his mother?'

'That's the biggie, ain't it?'

'What would you do?'

'In your place?'

'Yes'.

'Lie, probably. He's had enough shit to handle these past couple of weeks. Especially at his age.'

'But he's going to have to know sometime. Soon.'

She reached and clasped his arm. 'Eddie, you're too straightforward. Normally I like that in a man. It's rare. But you don't have to be a hundred percent honest with a hundred percent of people a hundred percent of the time. It might make *you* feel better, but the other party can be left wondering what hit them.'

'You've been reading my mind and absorbing my personality while I was asleep, haven't you?'

She shrugged. 'There are just no angles to you. Your dead straight. Sometimes a person needs angles just to get through life.'

Eddie flexed a bicep and pointed to his elbow. 'Angle.' He tilted his head until his ear touched his shoulder. 'Angle.'

Laura laughed. 'You're crazy. Make the best of your good mood. Tough times ahead.'

'Easy times. I can fix anything today. Easy. Watch me.'

'I will. From a front row seat.'

Eddie called Campbell Ogilvie, then rang his sister. He then phoned Charles Tunney and Broga Cates. By midday the wheels were in motion for him to become Kim's guardian on an interim basis, until the formalities could be completed. The only thing Campbell Ogilvie needed was Kim's confirmation of what he wanted.

In the whirl of tests and doctors and comings and goings, Eddie had not yet spent time alone with his nephew. When everything was lined up, Eddie asked for fifteen minutes of privacy.

He settled by Kim's bed, smiling. 'It's funny to see your face moving,' he said.

Kim looked puzzled. Eddie said, 'Well not literally. I mean it's not sliding from side to side or anything. Your eyes are open. You're talking. You're eating. It feels like weeks I've been sitting here looking at the quietest boy I've ever seen.'

'I never knew I had an uncle.'

'I never knew I had a nephew.'

Kim watched him. 'Have you any other nephews?'

Eddie shook his head.

'Nieces?'

'I'm totally nieceless. As far as I know.'

'It's a strange feeling,' Kim said.

'It is.'

'Are you my, my father's brother?'

'Your mother's. Your biological mother, I mean.'

'My real mother.'

Eddie sensed Kim did not want any flannel about the importance of his adoptive parents and how they'd always be his true father and mother. 'Your real mother,' Eddie said.

'Is she dead?'

'No. She's in Newmarket looking after our mother who is very ill; too ill for your mother to leave her. When she found out about you, she called me right away and we decided I should come here while she stayed with mother.' Eddie knew what might be coming next. Ogilvie had told him about his first appeal to Marie.

Kim said, 'What's my mother's name?'

'Marie.'

'How old is she?'

'Twenty seven.'

Kim looked at the ceiling. 'She was only three years older than I am when I was born.'

Eddie watched him. Kim turned his head to look at Eddie. 'It must have been awful hard for her. Tell her I'm sorry.'

Eddie felt a jolt of anger and a lump in his throat at the same time and had to batten down his reaction. 'You've nothing to be sorry for, Kim. We've all got choices, even at fourteen or fifteen. She took a chance.'

'With my father?'

'Yes.' Eddie was conscious he was getting out of his ground.

'Do you know my father?'

'No, I don't.'

'He must have been young too. Does your sister know where he is?'

'I don't think so.'

'Did your dad stop them seeing each other?'

'I don't know. I wasn't living with them back then.'

Kim looked at him. 'Did you not know about me when I was born?'

'I didn't know until Saturday night that you even existed.'

'You don't look very much older than twenty-seven, yourself.'

Eddie smiled. 'I'm thirty. Almost over the hill.'

'Did you leave home young, then? To make your fortune?'

'Kind of. Still waiting for the fortune though.'

'Mister Ogilvie told me you're a jockey.'

'That's right. Over jumps.'

'I've got a pony called Crystal. She's crap at jumping, though. But she's tough. She keeps on and on.'

'Many females do.'

Kim smiled, then laughed and his eyes sparkled. 'What's it like riding a racehorse?'

'It's like sitting on a rocket ship.'

'On it or in it?'

'On it.'

'That would be a good feeling.'

'It is. Would you like to try it?'

'Would they let me? With my head?'

'I'll talk them into it.'

Kim stared at the ceiling again. 'Are you going home now?'

'No. I'm staying here with you.'

Kim looked at him. 'How long for?'

'Until you're better and they discharge you.'

'Will you be able to visit me at the home some time?'

'What home?'

'The children's home.'

'You're not going to any children's home. No way. Unless you want to.'

'Where am I going? Mister Ogilvie said father had arranged boarding school for me.'

'Do you want to go to boarding school?'

'No. Not right now, anyway.'

'Well you're not going there either then.'

Kim sat up. 'Where will I be going?'

'It's your choice, but I've got plenty room at my place and there's a yard full of racehorses and mostly happy lads and lasses, and a slightly batty trainer called Charles Tunney, and about seven hundred acres of fields and woods and gallops. And I'm sure we can find a box for Crystal.'

'What about your job?'

'Plenty room in my car too when I'm going to the races. I'd be grateful for your company.'

'You're not kidding me?'

'I never kid with family.'

Kim watched him. Eddie told him to take some time and think about it, talk it over with Mister Ogilvie.

Kim nodded. 'I will. He's been very good to me, Mister Ogilvie. I've been lucky. I've been unlucky, then I've been lucky. It's funny how things sometimes work, isn't it?'

FORTY-EIGHT

They left hospital first thing Friday morning and walked across the car park to the Audi. Kim was impressed by it and Eddie promised he'd teach him to drive as soon as he was old enough. When they joined the southbound motorway Kim sat quietly, looking to the west as the lake district fells gradually began to line the horizon.

'Your farm's near here, isn't it?' Eddie asked.

'Not far,' he said, still gazing at the ragged line of hills.

'Do you want to go there before we head for my place?'

Kim was silent for a few moments. 'I do and I don't, if you know what I mean.'

'I know what you mean.'

'I've been feeling a kind of, a sad sort of longing for it in the past few days. Since I started feeling better. It's hard to explain. When I started feeling better, I started feeling worse. Sad and kind of lost, I suppose.'

'Grief's a strong, strong thing. It can be like a hand on your throat or in your stomach, or both. I wish I could tell you it'll go away soon, but I can't. Everybody's different.'

Kim gazed at the fells. 'The odd thing is, I haven't been thinking all that much about my father. It feels like a kind of grief for the farm and the hills and the fields and trees and Crystal...'

'That was your whole life, Kim. All you knew was there. It's natural to grieve for it. I was brought up not far from here myself. It's beautiful country. And it's just as fine where we're going,

Shropshire. A different kind of beauty, softer. But you'll like it. I know you will.'

'Mister Ogilvie said that when I'm twenty-one, I can maybe buy the farm back again, for myself.'

'No reason you couldn't. None at all. I'll still be under forty by that time and maybe I'll come and work for you.'

Kim turned to him. 'What about setting up our own racing stable!'

Eddie smiled. 'Good idea. You'll be the jockey by then. I could retire and take up training. Maybe I'll finally make that fortune I set out to make all those years ago.'

'We can both make our fortune! We can be partners!'

Eddie laughed, then quickly turned serious and determined looking. He held out his hand, 'It's a deal, partner!'

Kim shook it, then settled in his seat, gazing ahead. 'Let's make some plans,' he said.

FORTY-NINE

When they reached the yard, dusk was closing in. The quadrangle made up of stable-boxes looked soft and murky under the lights set above each door. Horses watched from most of the open half-doors. One neighed when it saw Kim. He smiled. 'That's Kumbaya,' Eddie said, 'I think he likes you.'

'Can I stroke him?'

'Sure.'

Kim walked to the corner box and Kumbaya began nodding as he approached. Slowly he raised a hand to the chestnut's cheek. The animal extended the range of its nodding until it moved like a rocking horse. 'You only need to hold your hand there,' Eddie said, 'looks like he wants to do the scratching himself.'

Eddie watched him for a minute, dredging his memory for a taste of how it felt to be twelve years old, just through the gateway of life and still on an early section of the path, the straight part, unsullied by anything you had done. Kim had been hurt, but not yet by his own hand. Eddie envied him and feared for him at the same time.

'Come on, Kim. Let's get in and get organized. We can come down for evening stables and meet all the horses and most of the lads.'

Upstairs, in the flat, Eddie was pleased to see that Charles had arranged a bed and some furniture for the spare room. Kim stood looking at it.

'You've got a wardrobe with nothing in it,' Eddie said. 'What do you say to a Christmas shopping spree in London soon?'

'I've never been to London. I'd like to see it. Can we go to Buckingham Palace?'

'We can go wherever you like, Kim. Wherever you like. You got enough clothes in that bag for the next day or two?'

Kim hefted the black bag by the handles. 'Sure. I usually always wear the same clothes anyway. We all do. It's called the Pareto Principle. We wear twenty percent of our clothes eighty percent of the time.'

Eddie smiled as he went to the kitchen to fill the kettle, 'So that's what they're teaching in schools these days, eh? I used to get algebra. Hated it.'

Kim followed him. 'I read about it. They didn't teach me it. It applies to lots of things. We play with twenty percent of our games eighty percent of the time. Twenty percent of customers are responsible for eighty percent of profits for most businesses. Would you say that twenty percent of trainers provide eighty percent of your rides?'

Eddie held the kettle under the gushing water. 'I think that'd be about right. And about twenty percent of the horses I ride bring about eighty percent of my winners. Hey, that's a bloody good rule that, what's it called again?'

'The Pareto Principle.'

'Nice one. You like stuff like that?'

'I like problems, figuring them out.'

'Well most people hate problems so I'd bet that twenty percent of boys solve eighty percent of problems.'

Kim smiled and drummed on the worktop with his hands, finishing with a flourish.

'You like drumming? Music?' Eddie asked.

'I like rhythmical things. Running, trotting on Crystal, swimming, that kind of stuff.'

Eddie rinsed a coffee mug. 'You ought to see me swimming…rhythmical's the last thing you'd call it.'

Eddie's phone rang. It was Matt Nash.

'Eddie, all well?'

'For now Matt, yes. How are you?'

'Counting the hours. Shitting myself in case the big horse steps on a stone.'

'Well, you can't keep him in his box.'

'Unfortunately. That's why I called. Just checking you're okay for that final piece of fast work on him on Monday?'

'Can't wait. I'll be bringing a friend, if you don't mind,' Eddie said.

Matt chuckled. 'Rebecca perchance?'

'Well, she might be there too but I'm bringing my nephew.'

'Didn't know you had one.'

'Neither did I. It's a long story. I'll tell you on Monday.'

'See you then.'

Eddie made a few more calls to confirm he'd be back riding next day at Uttoxeter and managed to get two definites from trainers who'd been holding for him. Kim, watching, looked worried. Eddie put a hand on his shoulder. 'Don't worry, I won't be going anywhere without you. You're coming racing with me tomorrow and Laura's got a runner there too so we'll see her as well.'

Kim pulled that steadily glowing smile again and Eddie was getting to recognize it coming on. He ruffled Kim's hair and took him down to meet Charles and the staff and the horses.

That evening, Eddie cooked his first proper meal for as long as he could remember.

Kim asked about every horse in the yard. He'd remembered the names of those he'd been particularly keen on and Eddie told him of their racing history and their characters and watched Kim concentrate with an intensity he'd never seen in anyone.

Kim watched TV for a while. Eddie sat reading the *Racing Post*, checking the form of his rivals for next day. When the ten o'clock news came on. Kim got up from where he'd been lying on the rug.

'Is it okay if I go to bed now?'

'Sure it is. Tired?'

Kim nodded. 'It's been a long day.'

'It has. Want me to come in and sit with you for a while once you're settled down?'

'No thanks. I'll be okay.'

'Good'.

'No offence,' Kim said.

'None taken. Come here.'

Kim went to stand by the side of Eddie's chair. Eddie ruffled the boy's thick dark hair. 'Good night, nephew.'

Kim moved behind the chair and ruffled Eddie's hair. 'Good night, uncle.'

Eddie laughed. Kim headed for his room. 'Hey!' Eddie called.

Kim turned. 'Don't call me uncle. Makes me feel old.'

Kim walked slowly back to stand in front of him. 'Okay. But don't call me nephew. Makes me feel young.' Kim offered his hand, 'Deal?'

Laughing again, Eddie shook it.

As soon as Kim left the room, the place felt oddly empty to Eddie. He, who for much of his life had wanted solitude, was already missing a boy he hardly knew. His thoughts went to Marie and what she was missing and his emotions grew so turbulent that Rebecca's face loomed in his mind, in a bridal veil…a mother for Kim if his own didn't want him.

Rebecca had been delighted earlier when he called to tell her about Kim coming home with him. Whether she'd be the motherly type was another matter, he supposed, then slapped himself with the rolled up newspaper. 'Snap out of it! You're going crazy.'

But he looked forward to seeing her again. He hadn't told Kim yet, but he planned to take him to London after racing tomorrow. They'd pick up Rebecca and have dinner, then stay over and do some Christmas shopping on the Sunday. That would be a nice surprise for him.

One thing Eddie did recall of his twelve-year-old self, women who looked like Rebecca had blown him away. He smiled, anticipating Kim's reaction.

FIFTY

Under normal circumstances, Ben Turco would not have been happy to be back in New York City after so many years. But getting lost among eight million people, three thousand miles away from whoever maimed Philip Grimond, held a lot of appeal right now.

They'd taken a while to ship his computer equipment across to this flat on Wall Street. Turco considered the high rent a good investment as the flat was two blocks north of the communications network for the Stock Exchange, and Turco thought that network might provide his next profitable challenge.

It would be his biggest test yet, but he knew that without the worry of being stalked by Grimond's assailant, he could relax and concentrate on it. Rubbing his hands and smiling widely Turco sat down at his desk and switched on his screen.

John Klemperer, an employee of the airline that had flown Turco to New York, sat in a Brooklyn bar, nervously drinking beer. Before Klemperer finished his drink, a short Chinese man joined him. Unsure of the protocol on these occasions, Klemperer offered a drink. It was politely refused as the man drew from the inside pocket of his black suit an envelope containing five hundred dollars. He gave it to Klemperer who then gave him a much smaller white envelope. Inside it was a single piece of A4 paper, which listed the New York address and telephone number of Benjamin J. Turco.

At Uttoxeter, Eddie rode Laura's horse Achilles to finish second in the novice 'chase. Kim was disappointed his uncle hadn't won but he tried not to let it show. The excitement of the racecourse, the sights and sounds, the smells, the crowds roaring at the end of each race, the cries of the bookies, the wild optimism of the stable lads, the stirring sight of swollen-veined, steaming horses close up, and the presence of his uncle in full jockey's gear talking to all the obviously important people - Kim felt almost overcome at times.

Laura looked after him when Eddie was in the changing room. Laura sought Kim's help to saddle Achilles, and she promised Kim that someday soon he could come and ride Achilles on the beach.

One person Kim didn't like was the huge man who came lumbering toward them in the car park. He'd been waiting by Eddie's car, leaning on it, and as soon as he'd seen the three of them coming, he'd stood up and headed straight for them.

Kim felt vulnerable watching him approach, a giant wearing strange clothes and a big hat. He'd grabbed Eddie by the shoulder, almost pleading for Eddie to listen, to let him tell him what really happened with somebody called Grimond.

Eddie took him away and they'd spoken so quietly then that Kim hadn't heard anything. Laura didn't seem to like the man either, though she didn't mention it and when Eddie came back she just kissed him goodbye and did the same to Kim.

When they got in the car Kim said, 'Was that man angry with you?'

Eddie smiled. 'The other way around, Kim, I was angry with him. He let me down badly and he was just apologizing.'

'Are you his boss or something?'

'I'm not his boss. I'm nobody's boss and that's the best way to be. His name's Tiny Delaware, he's ...'

'Tiny!'

'That's what they call him. A sort of joke. Anyway, he's a bit of a character. You'll find a few Tiny Delawares if you stay in racing for a while. It's a bit like the law of the jungle, people get by on what they can, survive on their wits, dull as they might be at times. In racing there's always somebody more stupid, more gullible, no matter what your level is.'

'Did Tiny think you were gullible?'

'He did. And he was right. That's what Tiny was apologizing about.'

'And did you accept his apology?'

Eddie didn't tell Kim that the big man apologized out of fear. He was afraid someone sympathetic to Eddie might have arranged the maiming of Grimond and he didn't want the same fate. 'Yep, I accepted it. No hard feelings. Now guess where we're going?'

Kim looked up at him and just shook his head in curiosity.

'London! London Town!' Eddie shouted and tapped out a drum roll on the steering wheel.

Kim smiled, his eyes sparkling. 'What for?'

'There's somebody there I want you to meet. And I want her to meet you. You'll be impressed, Kim; guaranteed. She's very beautiful!'

Kim blushed and Eddie laughed and spun the wheel to head for the gate.

Shortly after they'd driven out of the car park, a relieved Tiny reached the exit on foot and stood with his thumb out. He never had to wait long for a lift at the races. Most of the regulars knew him, and sure enough, he hadn't been there two minutes when a big Merc pulled up. He didn't recognize the blokes in it as he ducked and squeezed himself into the back. Little guys for such a big car. He smiled and said, 'Thanks, fellas!' But they didn't reply, and when Tiny saw their reflections in the rear-view mirror, he put their silence down to the fact that they probably didn't speak English.

FIFTY-ONE

Kim was almost as impressed with the lobby of the Dorchester Hotel as he'd been with Buckingham Palace; all marble and pillars, soft lights and giant plants and music, which seemed part of the air around them.

When Rebecca came out of the lift, Eddie nudged Kim and nodded in her direction as she swung toward them in high heels and black pencil dress. Kim took in the cleavage and the knees, the tan and the bright smile and the sparkling necklace and, as she reached them, the wonderful scent, and as Eddie stood up, Kim jumped to his feet to find himself at breast height, blushing and wanting to be ten years older or to escape immediately. He resolved it by sitting down again. Eddie, watching his face, smiled and resisted ruffling the boy's hair, a habit he was already trying to get out of.

'You must be Kim?'

'Yes, ma'am.'

'I'm pleased to meet you. You're much better looking than your uncle,'

Kim shook her hand, speechless. 'Then again,' she said, 'he's been kicked around a fair bit. He's bruised and battered. You look brand new, and I'm predicting right now that once you've reached your uncle's age, there'll be a trail of broken hearts behind you as long as this lobby.'

'I hope not.' Kim said.

'And I hope not too. I was kidding. But don't get hooked on the first beautiful girl you meet. It's a big world out there. There are about three billion women in it.'

'That's a lot,' Kim said.

She put a hand on his shoulder. 'I'm scaring you now, aren't I?'

Kim shrugged and looked at his shoes. Eddie hugged Rebecca. 'You look absolutely stunning.'

'Thank you. I wanted to be at my best for two handsome gentlemen. Now, I've booked a table for dinner. Shall we eat?'

Eddie turned to Kim. 'Hungry?'

Kim shrugged again. He dreaded sitting at a table with this beautiful woman in this posh place. He pictured the food he'd be certain to drop on his shirt or on the floor, and he wanted to run through the main doors and not stop until he cleared the city.

But he got through the meal in one piece. They'd tried to keep involving him in the conversation, but he felt happiest when they became wrapped up in their own words and forgot him and he could just be an observer.

The room was big and crowded. Three tables away, behind Eddie, sat four Chinese men. Kim noticed how one of them kept watching Rebecca and how she'd sometimes glance at him, and he was relieved Eddie couldn't see another man eyeing up his girl.

After dinner, Rebecca said goodbye, telling Kim she had to meet her sister. Eddie and Kim went to a smaller hotel. They lay in the twin beds in the darkness with the sounds of London nightlife rising from the street. Kim said, 'Did Rebecca go away because I'm here?'

'Rebecca's got a busy day tomorrow. Anyway, she knows it's the boys' night out.'

Kim was silent for a minute then said quietly, 'I wouldn't have minded, Eddie, if you'd stayed with her.'

'I know you wouldn't but I wanted to be with you tonight. Stop worrying. I'll have lots of time with Rebecca in the future and you will too.'

Silence for another minute, then, 'Are you going to marry her?'

'Do you think I should?'

'I don't know.'

'Would you marry her if you were in my position?'

'Emmm…I don't suppose I really know her.'

It was Eddie's turn to be quiet.

Eddie faded off to sleep, but Kim lay wide-eyed into the early hours listening to his uncle snoring lightly, smiling at the sound, as he watched the ceiling fan skip slowly in and out of shadow.

Even if the ceiling above Kim had been open to the sky, what stars he might have seen would have been faint, dulled by the pollution of light rising from the big city. But from a field of frosted stubble deep in the Staffordshire countryside, the view above was heart-lifting. The stars glittered so brilliantly in the blackness, a man might imagine he could see the very edges of them.

Simple fellow though he was at times, it was a sight Tiny Delaware would have appreciated, especially as he was normally nearer the stars than most mortals. But although Tiny lay on his back in that field, close to a blackthorn hedge, he could see nothing. Pain and shock had thrown the safety switch in his brain, shutting it down.

The moon was full. Silver light from it made Tiny's oozing head gleam in the wettest places. His scalp had been removed comparatively neatly considering it had been sliced off with a sword.

As Tiny moaned and tried to turn over on the damp cold ground, an old dogfox following the blood scent, finally found the oddest of meals. He licked twice at the congealed mess on the inside of the scalp, then took the whole thing in his mouth and trotted off along the line of the hedge.

FIFTY-TWO

Eddie and Kim went Christmas shopping on Sunday. Eddie gave Kim one hundred pounds to buy presents, promising the reluctant boy he could pay it back when he rode his first winner. He was rewarded once again with that slow-burning smile.

They reached home in time for evening stables and Kim went round all the horses with Charles. Eddie, phone to his ear, talking to Laura, watched from his window on the top floor as the boy followed the trainer keenly from box to box. Eddie told Laura of their London trip.

Laura, wanting to move the conversation away from Rebecca, asked if Kim had got over the lumbering sight of Tiny Delaware bearing down on them on Saturday.

'He hasn't mentioned it again, but it's been on my mind on and off since. I feel like I've been stupid and gone rushing into things, again - big surprise - without thinking.'

Laura knew him well enough to stay quiet and let him talk it out.

'When Marie told me about Kim, everything else disappeared. I wanted him out of that hospital and looked after properly by somebody who cared for him. I conveniently forgot about all that shit with Grimond and Tiny and Matt and the Chinese. Just decided to assume it was all finished. Then the cops turn up asking questions. Then Tiny comes running at us like a madman. And here's me waiting to sign legal papers to become Kim's guardian. Here's me thinking that if the shit hits the fan again, I'll just sort it, just handle it the way I've always done. No thought for Kim. Only for myself. As ever. I'm an idiot, Laura.'

'You're what I said you were the other day. You're straight and clean. There are no angles to you. You do what you think is the best for people, not for yourself.'

'What about all this? The police mentioned a DNA test. What if they turn up on the doorstep at dawn? What if Grimond accuses me of the attack? What if old Lee Sung decides it ain't over after all and it's time he paid me back for the beating I gave him?'

'He'd have done that by now, Eddie, wouldn't he? There would have been no sense letting it run on, not for him. Think about it, they had another go with Matt when Samson's Curls lost, or won, or however you want to put it. But they never came near you. There hasn't been the hint of a threat, has there?'

'No, I suppose not. I just think I've ballsed this up big style. Look, Kim's on his way back upstairs. We're down at Matt's tomorrow morning early. Prince Simba has his last piece of work. I'll let you know how that goes, ok? Oh, and by the way, how are you? I'm so wrapped up in myself I haven't even asked how you are. I'm sorry.'

'Don't be so bloody daft. It's not a fifty-fifty trade off on who gets to talk. Give yourself a break, for God's sake. I'm your friend. I listen when you need listened to. I give advice when you need it, whether you like it or not. I love advice. Never take any myself, but I relish dishing it out. *Relish*, do you hear?'

Eddie laughed. Kim came through the door. Eddie was still laughing, and he gestured the smiling boy to come to him. 'Your aunt Laura's on the phone. Want to say hello?'

Kim took the phone and spent the next ten minutes babbling about what all his favourite horses were going to do, which races they would win. Eddie listened from the kitchen and felt something intangible squeezing his heart, and something fierce and angry damning his judgement in enticing an emotionally damaged child into a new life that could be blown to smithereens without warning.

FIFTY-THREE

Kim stood in the yard of Matt Nash watching Eddie being legged up on the big black Prince Simba who Kim decided was the finest creature he'd ever seen. Matt climbed aboard his chestnut hack and he and Eddie sat smiling down at Kim, who seemed unaware of the clip-clop of hooves behind him until Eddie nodded at the lad who held the brown gelding. Kim turned slowly and the lad offered him the reins and a helmet. Kim looked confused; he was about to tell the lad he was mistaken when Eddie said, 'Come on, Kim, up you get or we'll be late!'

Kim said, 'Me!' pointing to his chest.

Eddie and Matt said at the same time, 'Yes, you!'

As they walked the lanes and headed up toward the gallops, Kim sat higher than he ever had on a horse, this racehorse, albeit retired, and saw for miles over the hedgetops. And at that moment he became certain of two things: one, that this was the best morning of his life and, two, that like his uncle, he was going to be a jockey.

Prince Simba worked better than either Eddie or Matt expected, and they were convinced he would win the King George, barring accidents.

Eddie had three rides at Ludlow and he and Kim talked racing all the way there. Eddie was elated at the boy's interest. He felt his chance of ever being champion again had gone, but he would get as much satisfaction from grooming the boy to become one of the best.

Eddie's mounts finished second, third and unplaced and Kim was getting anxious to see him ride his first winner. 'Don't worry,' Eddie told him, 'might as well make it the big one on Friday.'

It was dark when they got back to the flat and while Kim took a hot bath, Eddie set to work making a curry. As the sauce neared boiling point Eddie thought he heard the downstairs door open, then the sound of Charles's footsteps.

The trainer knocked lightly on the top door and Eddie shouted, 'Come in, Charles.' He entered, grinning and carrying an almost square package, twice the size of a shoebox, gift wrapped in shiny berry-red. 'This came this morning and I know you don't get many Christmas presents.' Charles put it down on the worktop and leant over the curry pot to sniff. 'Smells nice.'

'Want some? There's plenty.'

'Maybe I will.'

'Good. Kim's in the bath. He'll be out in a minute. Pull up a chair and pour a drink.'

'Good idea. Want one?'

'Why not?'

Charles fixed whiskeys while Eddie got a knife and began opening the box, which he suspected had come from Rebecca. As he sliced through the broad tape he heard the sloshing of water next door as Kim stood up in the bath then the sound of his feet on the floor as he stepped out.

Inside the box were a fat blue vacuum flask and an audio tape. Puzzled, Eddie lifted them out. The flask felt full. A card hung from each item, tied with thin yellow twine. Eddie read the one dangling from the cup handle of the flask: 'Do what is required on Friday or you may end up without these …' The one on the tape said, '… and with this.'

He let Charles read them, then they looked at each other as though searching for the answer. Eddie carefully unscrewed the flask lid and held it below the light to peer inside. All he could see was dark liquid.

Kim came in, barefoot, jeans on, towelling his still wet torso. Drips from his hair fell on the tiles. Towel moving rhythmically across his back he watched as Eddie put the plug in the stainless steel sink and slowly emptied the flask. The liquid was clear; it flowed with the consistency of thick bleach. Halfway through the stream, a human tongue swam out followed by an eye. They circled in the gently swirling water.

Charles recoiled and sucked in a breath. Eddie looked at the organs. Kim stopped towelling and nudged Eddie who turned absent-mindedly, still holding the flask at an angle. Kim pointed to it, 'Look.' Perched on the rim of the flask was another eye. Quickly turning it upside down Eddie watched the eye drop with a plop in beside its companions. He and Charles stared in awe at the organs. Kim looked calm and curious.

'Grimond's,' Eddie said.

'What?' asked Charles.

'Tell you later.'

He held the see-through tape up to the light. All it read, apart from the dangling card, was C60. Eddie pulled the card off, slotted the tape into his deck and pressed play. Four seconds later it clicked and stopped.

'Wrong side,' he said.

He turned it over.

A pop song came from the speakers. It was vaguely familiar to Eddie and Charles but neither could name it. Eddie looked again at the card. The threat attached to the flask hadn't been hard to work out: 'you could end up without these'. He read the card from the tape as the song played and could make nothing of it: 'and with this'.

Kim had the towel around his neck now, holding the ends. Eddie said to him, 'Do you know the name of the song?' Kim told them it was called *Missing*.

Eddie looked again at the card and read it out: 'And with this. *Missing*.' He looked at Charles. 'With what missing, a tape?' Charles shrugged.

Kim reached for the card, and held it in his palm. 'I think it might not be the song. It could be the group's name.'

They waited.

Solemn-faced, Kim said, 'They're called, "Everything but the Girl".'

FIFTY-FOUR

Eddie ran for the phone and dialled Rebecca's number. After six rings she answered. 'Rebecca! Are you all right?'

'Yes.' She sounded subdued.

'Is anyone there with you?'

'No, Eddie.'

'Tell me what's happened.'

After a long pause she said, 'It's best if we don't see each other again.'

'Rebecca, tell me what's wrong?'

'I'll deal with it, Eddie. Please, it's best that way.' The sorrow in her voice seemed to deepen.

'Whatever it is we'll deal with it together. Now, please tell me what's happened.'

'Not over the phone. If I come to see you and tell you, will you promise to leave it to me? Will you promise to keep out of it?'

'Can you come now?'

'Promise me, first.'

'I can't promise. You know that! Whatever's happened has happened to both of us, not just you. Come on!'

Another pause. 'Eddie, you have Kim to look after now. You need to stay out of this.'

Eddie looked frustratedly at Charles and Kim. 'Tell me where you are, I'll come to you.'

'No! No, I'll come to you,' Rebecca said.

'Now?'

'Yes, now. I should be there in a couple of hours.'

'Okay. Please be careful.'

'I will.'

'Rebecca! Tell me one thing, a one word answer. Does this have something to do with the Triads?'

The silence answered him before she did. 'Yes.'

When he put the phone down Charles said, 'Well?'

'Can I come over to the house later?'

Charles glanced at Kim. 'Okay.'

When the trainer left, Eddie sat down. He looked at Kim who stood by the fireplace. Then Eddie covered his face with his hands and massaged his eyes, and sighed.

'Are you going to send me away?' Kim asked.

Eddie looked at him and said, 'Kim. I've made a total mess of everything. I didn't think anything through. All I wanted was to get you home. Mister Ogilvie wanted that too and I took advantage of that and pushed him for interim court orders and stuff, and I should have stopped and thought about it properly. I've ballsed things up and put you in danger, which is even worse.'

'How? How have you put me in danger? You did what you thought best for me, didn't you? You could have left me in that hospital and walked away, and you didn't, so whatever's happened can be fixed, can't it?'

Eddie rubbed his forehead, 'I don't know. It depends how much trouble Rebecca's in.'

'Do you know what kind of trouble it is?'

'I think it might be something to do with the men who sent the flask and the tape.'

'That was a threat to you, wasn't it, not Rebecca? And it said about Friday and that's the big race, isn't it?'

'It is. Look Kim, how would you feel about me calling Mister Ogilvie in the morning. I need to get his advice on how best to keep you safe and I need to tell him I wasn't straight with him. Otherwise he could get struck off. He could lose his business.'

'Do you think I'll need to go back to that home?'

Eddie got up and went to him and put an arm round his shoulders. 'I promise you this now, you won't be going back to that home. I promise.'

Kim looked up at him. 'Do those men know I'm here?'

'I don't know. They might.'

'Couldn't I go to Matt's for a while?'

'Matt's would be just about the last place I'd send you if it's the people I think it is.'

'Why are they after you? Can you say?'

Eddie sighed and looked to the ceiling.

'It's okay if you can't,' Kim said.

'Put your shoes on. I've got to explain to Charles and you're owed the same explanation. Let's go and see him.'

At the long pine table in Charles's kitchen, Eddie told them everything from the day he'd buried the headless corpse of Matt's dog. Kim hardly blinked throughout the whole tale. Eddie played down his part in rescuing Matt.

Charles smiled wearily and shook his head. 'It's just as well Broga Cates thinks you're a one-off, Eddie. He's right, of course, but most owners would run a mile from you. Broga finds all this stuff entertaining. I need to be frank with you, if it was down to me, you'd be on your way out tonight. I'm like my horses; routine's what I need, predictability. You live in a crazy world.'

'Charles, all I can say is that I never plan this stuff. It just happens to me,'

'That's what worries me most.'

'I'm sorry.'

'I know you are. And I wish I could help you.'

'I'll handle it, Charles.'

The trainer nodded slowly. Eddie turned to Kim. 'Will you sit with Charles for ten minutes? I need to make a call.'

'Okay.'

'All right with you, Charles? I won't be long. First step in sorting this out.'

'Good. Kim, want some supper?'

Eddie returned to the flat and dialled the Malloy stud. He pictured the phone ringing out in the dark hallway and Marie hurrying downstairs from that room he despised. The one his father died in. The one his mother had cocooned herself in to hide from the world.

'Hello?'

'Marie, it's Eddie.'

FIFTY-FIVE

In the flat, in the lamplight, Eddie and Kim waited for Rebecca. Eddie briefly considered asking Charles if Kim could stay the night in the house, but the trainer wanted no involvement in any of this, he'd made that clear. And Eddie wanted Kim close by anyway, well within protection range. Whatever Rebecca had to say, it wouldn't much matter if Kim heard it. Eddie had told him everything.

She arrived at 10.30 looking tired and worried. She wore blue jeans and a heavy black sweater, the first time Eddie had seen her dressed casually. As they hugged and kissed Kim went to fill the kettle, and Eddie told her that Kim knew everything so far. He mentioned the flask and the tape and he thought the surprised reaction she came up with seemed forced. Maybe because of the stress, thought Eddie, who sat with her on the couch. Kim settled in the chair, lower legs folded beneath him. All three held mugs of tea and Rebecca, in a resigned voice, began.

The story Rebecca told them was that her sister, Annelise, a gambling addict, owed a Triad more than two hundred thousand pounds.

Rebecca said she'd done all she could to help: paid Annelise's early debts, financed expensive treatment for her addiction, sweated blood to hide the facts from her sick mother and now it had come to nothing. Annelise was suicidal and the Triad latched onto Rebecca because of her association with racing, and with Eddie.

Eddie listened, trying to think at the same time, hoping to figure a way out of what he feared was coming. He said, 'Is it the same people who lent Matt the money? The ones who attacked him?'

Rebecca, tearful, nodded slowly. 'And did they know you had horses with Matt? Did they know he needed cash to keep his stable going?'

'Yes. My fault. I mentioned it to Annelise just by way of telling her I planned to buy into the business in March to help Matt out. But she took that information and ... and sold it to the Triad. They paid her for pulling another victim into their net and I felt awful about it. That's why I called you that night when they took Matt. That's why I enjoyed so much getting one back on the bastards!' She glanced quickly at Kim then Eddie. 'Sorry.'

Kim smiled. Eddie said, 'It's all right. Where is Annelise now?'

Rebecca sat stooped forward, elbows on knees, staring at the floor. 'She's at Mother's. I took her there earlier today. But I don't know how long she'll stay. If she's not within striking distance of a roulette table she panics.' She glanced at Eddie. 'The other night, when Matt thought he saw me going into the casino...'

Eddie said, 'Annelise?'

Rebecca nodded glumly then got to her feet. 'I've told you the tale and that's what I promised to do. Now it's best if I get back to Mother's, see if Annelise is still there. I'll call you when all this is over, Eddie.'

He stood up and reached for her, clasping a hand at the top of each arm and holding her, making her look straight at him. 'You're not going anywhere without me. You need to tell me exactly what the Triad wants.'

Rebecca went hard-eyed. 'I don't need to tell you anything. Not a thing.'

The sudden coldness hurt him, she could see it in his eyes. She softened again, reaching to stroke his hair. 'I'm sorry, Eddie, but you mean a lot to me too. I realize you want to protect me, but I want to protect you too and this is the best way to do it.'

Kim watched.

Eddie held her tighter. 'Rebecca, listen, tell me what it is these people want!'

She gazed at him, 'They want me to make you do something and I said no. I told them no matter what they threaten me or Annelise with I'll never ask it.'

'Ask. It's for me to decide.'

She stared at him. 'They want you to pull Prince Simba in the King George on Friday.'

Involuntarily, he let go of her arms. He hesitated a few seconds then said quietly, 'I can't do that.'

Now Rebecca gripped his arms. 'I know you can't! That's why I would never ask you!'

He eased himself away and sat on the arm of Kim's chair. Kim put a hand on his shoulder. Eddie looked at her. 'What's the ultimatum? What happens if I don't?'

'That doesn't come into it, Eddie, because you're not going to.'

'Rebecca, tell me what they've threatened you with.'

Again she hesitated then said, 'They said they'd take Annelise to Hong Kong and force her to work as a prostitute...and me too.'

'Nice men,' Eddie said. 'I think it's time we brought the police in.'

'Eddie, listen, the Triads have as much fear of the police as you have of riding a seaside donkey. Try and find the name of the last Triad member to be convicted of anything. Nobody will testify against them.'

'I'll testify,' Eddie said. 'You can testify, tell the police about the threats.'

'And what will they do? They'll interview Lee Sung and his gang who will laugh in their faces and deny it.'

'Well they won't be able to deny Matt's missing finger, or his scarred hand or his dead dog!'

Rebecca shook her head slowly as though she thought Eddie naive. 'And you think Matt will testify? You think he'll stand up in court and admit his business was so far down the pan he took money from Chinese moneylenders? That he tipped them a horse you had given him which got beat? Do you think he'll do all that standing up there in the dock with these guys terrifying the life out of him? Do you think he'll go home and sleep well in his bed after that? Do you think you're entitled to ask Matt to do that just for me, because I don't?'

'Okay, okay. We'll find another way. We'll find another way, but as my old friend Ben Turco would say, we ain't pulling no horse.'

Rebecca sat on the couch. 'There is no way round it, Eddie.'

'We'll keep you safe, don't worry.'

'Who's we?'

'Me. Me and whoever I can get.'

'What about Kim?'

'I wouldn't put Kim at risk any more than I would you. I'll fix it. Trust me.'

She stared at him. 'Eddie, there is no fixing it. I know these people. Ever since Annelise got tied up with them I've been trying to find ways of beating them. It can't be done! Sure, we can have our little jabs at them like we did that night in Wardour Street, but that's it. You can win a round but no way can you win the match.'

Eddie kept smiling.

'Stop smiling so patronisingly! You think I'm overreacting, don't you? Let me tell you a few things about the Triads. There are hundreds of them all over the world. They have one goal in life: to make money. They're like robots. They don't do human feelings...sympathy and regret. They function twenty-four hours a day like a bloody big criminal machine.

'They're into protection rackets, labour gangs, illegal bookmaking, loan-sharking, drugs, illegal immigration, counterfeit currency, tax evasion, money laundering, insurance and credit card fraud and God knows what else.

'They're sadistic, ritualistic, cruel. They use swords and meat cleavers. One of their tricks is the slicing of the main muscles. Slashing of the scalp is optional but they've threatened me with that too.

'Now if they're not picking on people like me and Annelise, the Triads are fighting among themselves. They all have their own lodges, their own names. Lee Sung's little lot are known in English as The Third Degree, and from what I've learnt over the past year you don't mess with them. I'm not asking you to pull that horse, Eddie, all I'm saying is don't look for an alternative because there isn't one.'

Eddie watched her catch her breath, then said, 'So what did you plan to do?'

'The only thing I can, leave the country.'

'You and Annelise?'

'That's right.'

'When?'

'Tomorrow. Fly out somewhere warm. Hopefully lose ourselves in the Christmas holiday crowds.'

Eddie stood up. 'Given all that superhuman stuff you just rhymed off, they're not going to have much trouble finding you, are they?'

She stared at him.

Kim spoke. 'What good will it do them, these Triads, if Prince Simba loses?'

'They'll use their illegal bookmaking side to offer the horse at a bigger price than the normal bookies, Kim,' Eddie told him. 'It's one of the biggest betting races of the season. They could take a fortune on Prince Simba.'

Kim frowned. Eddie and Rebecca talked, almost forgetting Kim was there until he said, 'If the Triads fight a lot among themselves why don't we get one on our side?'

They turned to him. Kim went on, 'Couldn't you contact another Triad and tell them to bet thousands with these other ones on Prince Simba, especially if they're going to be offering a bigger price? You'd be doing them a favour, wouldn't you? And then you could ask them to protect you from the other Triad.'

A smile grew slowly on Eddie's face and he turned to look at Rebecca. 'What do think of that then?' he asked proudly. She didn't look much happier. 'I don't know.'

Eddie said. 'Do you know of another Triad, a rival one?'

She seemed to stare at the wall for a long time. 'I know someone who does, the girl who got me all the information on The Third Degree.'

'Do you think that would be the sort of proposal she'd be willing to take to another Triad?' Eddie asked.

Rebecca seemed puzzled. 'I can ask,' she said. 'But what if Prince Simba lost?'

Eddie shrugged. 'Luck of the draw. They'd have to be made aware of that before we started.'

'Then what are we offering them that they couldn't take advantage of anyway if they wanted?'

Eddie smiled. 'We're offering them the precious piece of knowledge that the horse will not be pulled when their rivals believe it will be.'

Rebecca stared at the floor. Eddie went to his nephew and shook his hand. 'You're a genius.'

FIFTY-SIX

From atop Prince Simba, Eddie looked to his right at the many thousands crammed into the Kempton stands. Their judgement as racing experts was on the line, their cash down, their champion chosen. The excitement seemed tangible. He could feel a building wave of it as the commentator named each parading horse and told of its accomplishments - Gladiators entering the arena. He knew the choice of the masses was the big black horse that carried him.

He thought of Rebecca; she and Annelise had been promised protection from the rival Triad. Trouble was, none could be trusted. But Eddie could see no other way out. The best they could hope for was rival gangs fighting themselves to exhaustion over settling the huge bets.

As Eddie passed the winning post now in this slow parade he raised a hand as promised, to friends at the track, and to Rebecca, hidden away in a tiny cottage on the North Devon coast, watching on TV. Kim waited in the stands with Laura Gilpin. Laura had no runners at Kempton but had come to see Eddie try to win the big one.

Matt Nash had offered to look after Kim during the race, but Eddie rejected that quickly, and maybe, on reflection, harshly. But he felt resentful of Matt now. Happy for the ride on Prince Simba, but angry at the way Matt had manipulated him into all this. The deepest resentment, as ever with Eddie, was reserved for himself and the way he bulldozed through life and through people without stopping to think.

He remained uneasy about Kim being out of his sight. He'd wanted the boy to go to Devon with Rebecca, but Kim had pleaded to be at Kempton. And Eddie's ego, his need for Kim's admiration, had eased him into agreement.

That bothered him too.

Then again, if the Triads were tracking Rebecca, it was best if Kim avoided her.

Eddie squeezed his eyes closed, trying to force out all the negativity. This was the King George VI Steeplechase. Arkle had won it, the greatest steeplechaser in history.

Many champions had won it. To ride the winner was to imprint yourself in the history books. Time to be positive.

The lads loosed their grips and stepped away. No more walking. The horses launched themselves, uncoiling into action to canter to the start. Eddie gathered the reins of the big black beast and as he passed a fence, smiled at the panning camera and winked for Rebecca, safe in her cottage by the sea.

Pulling his goggles down, Eddie urged Prince Simba into line along with the others and waited for the starter to hit the lever.

The power surge from a standing start to gallop needed all his concentration. The first fence came up quickly. He had to find a clear yard of birch to jump.

With the field so tightly packed, the horses leaned on each other, raising their excitement and speed while jockeys fought for a position for the first jump. The horses either side of Eddie were of different height. Tobin's stirrup irons clanked against Eddie's, adding a strange morse code to the meshing noise of hoofbeats, clinking bits, shouts for room and early cheering from the stands. On Eddie's inside O'Rourke's stirrup pressed so hard onto Eddie's shin, the pain made him shout for 'daylight'.

Prince Simba was keen, the type that did not merely aim to get over a jump, he wanted to devour it. The moment he saw the line of black birch he instinctively quickened at it and became airborne a couple of strides earlier than his rivals.

The pair soared past four horses, landed running and within seconds had broken away to lead.

Prince Simba attacked the fences, stretching fifteen lengths clear of the pack. Eddie knew the jockeys behind would think he'd gone mad but he trusted his pace judgment.

Prince Simba's jumping had been flawless. He'd settled into the perfect stride pattern, breathing evenly, galloping rhythmically, but Eddie knew the challenges would come.

At the farthest point from the winning post, the last of the open ditches loomed. As Eddie counted the horse in, a photographer stood up from a squatting position, distracting Prince Simba.

The horse missed a stride and belted the guard rail of the ditch.

His head went earthwards; Eddie slipped a foot of rein and sat back in the saddle as his mount stretched his long neck, trying to maintain equilibrium. Eddie saw the horse's tail, a sight that normally signals the world turning upside down. But Prince Simba scrambled along the grass, and from deep beneath his gut found a leg from somewhere to save him from somersaulting at thirty-eight miles per hour.

Four horses passed the sliding pair and the race had gone from won to lost.

Eddie had to give Prince Simba time to fill his lungs, to regain his breathing rhythm, his balance, his confidence.

Momentum would have to be carefully rebuilt.

Steadily, he and Prince Simba began fighting their way back into it. Two horses fought for the lead jumping the second last fence. There was just an outside chance that Eddie could sneak up on them unseen as the two jockeys were locked in battle, drifting toward the middle of the last fence as energy drained and desperation grew.

Eddie resisted the impulse to go for broke. Kempton's run in is one of the shortest in the country. His only chance lay in surprise, and should he mistime the last fence, all would be lost.

The fence came. The horse leapt. He landed within two lengths of the leading pair who continued to drift across the course in the head-down drive to the line. Prince Simba battled. Eddie rowed and kicked, almost crying with desperation and effort.

The red-ringed winning post seemed to move toward them

Eddie screamed in his mount's left ear, stirring a final surge from the frightened animal, and neither horse nor rider heard the primal sounds from the throats of thirty thousand race fans, as they won by a head.

Riding back to the winner's enclosure, Eddie scanned the ranks of upturned faces. Rebecca had told him that the Triad who'd been given the correct information, had promised they'd have men at the course whose very presence would deter their rivals.

They'd promised to trail Eddie discreetly to ensure his safety. But Eddie had asked Laura to keep Kim away from the celebrations. Matt, leading the horse in, punched the air so often it looked like some crazy form of one-handed shadow boxing.

Matt knew the score. He'd have to look after himself. But Matt wasn't worried; Eddie was in the frame for this, as far as Matt was concerned. What would Lee Sung want with Matt?

Eddie got changed and left the weighing room, the 'well dones' echoing along the corridor, following him out.

On the weighing room steps, he looked around: no Orientals. Maybe they could see him. He turned in the direction of the car park. A hand gripped his shoulder.

He spun. It was McCarthy. The big security man said, 'That's just about the quickest I've ever seen you move.'

'Jeez, talk about the long arm of the law!'

'Believe it or not, that is what's reaching out for you at this very minute. Figuratively speaking.'

Eddie was wary. 'How figuratively?'

'They want to talk to you again. At a little more length this time, I'm afraid. And, as the saying goes, at their place, not yours.'

'When?'

'Now.'

'Why?'

'Why now or why do they want to speak to you?'

'Both.'

'Well, remember Grimond, the tongueless and eyeless Grimond?'

'The tongueless, eyeless, bent, blackmailing Grimond?'

'The very same. The shortage of oral and visual organs no longer troubles him. He died in hospital last night.'

'Can't say I'll be sending flowers.'

'Well maybe you'd like to send some to your old buddy Tiny Delaware, though a wig would probably be more useful.'

'Pardon?'

'Tiny's in hospital too. They found him lying under a hedge in Staffordshire without his scalp.'

Eddie looked stunned.

'The day you were seen talking to Grimond, you were also seen talking to Tiny.'

'I saw him at Cheltenham too. He was trying to apologize.'

'That's the day they got Tiny.'

'What did he tell the police?'

'Very little. He's terrified.'

'Did he mention the Chinese to them?'

McCarthy glanced past him and said, 'Ask them.'

Eddie turned and saw the two cops, Blackstock and Reid walking toward him.

Well, he thought, if the Triad guys are waiting in the car park there should be some fun and games now.

FIFTY-SEVEN

They allowed Eddie a phone call. He rang Laura. 'Phil Grimond died last night.'

'My God!'

'The police, as they say, have asked me to help them with their enquiries, on their own patch, up in Stafford. I don't know when I'll be done there.'

'They think you had something to do with it!'

'No. No, they don't. They're just struggling. They already came to see me, remember?'

'Oh, yes, that night you were late back to the hospital. Look, do you want me to take Kim home with me?'

'Would you mind? I'll drive up and get him as soon as they let me out.'

'Of course. I promised he could ride Achilles on the beach, so you might have to stay over until morning.'

'The way the shit's bouncing off the fan here, I might not be there until morning. Tell Kim I miss him and I'll see him soon.'

'Do you want me to say you're with the police?'

'Yes. Tell him. No point treating him as though he's six.'

'Okay. See you later.'

'You're a good woman.'

'I know.'

Eddie laughed.

In the interview room at Stafford police station, Eddie soon realized that the good cop bad cop routine had been cancelled.

184

Blackstock's jollity from that first night had gone. He was all business and stern questions.

Eddie stayed patient and civil. He offered to take a DNA test to rule him out of the Grimond attack scene.

'We'll arrange that when the time's right,' Reid said.

Eddie shrugged. Reid sighed and said, 'I need a smoke.' He left Eddie with Blackstock

'Have you remembered who Grimond was working with on the photo-finish fraud?' Blackstock asked.

'I never forgot. I just didn't know. Still don't.'

'You believe Grimond was the top man?'

'No reason to think he wasn't.'

'He had to have runners working for him.'

'I'm sure he did.'

'Did he seem the type to be some sort of technical mastermind?'

'I didn't know the guy. He set me up easily, so he was smarter than me, though that's not saying much.'

'He had no technical background beyond basic PC skills.'

'And photography. And a flair for blackmail.'

They worked on him for over an hour. Eddie stayed cool throughout, kept Turco out of it, and when the merry-go-round got worn out with the same questions over and over, they let him go.

Eddie left, cursing them. He'd missed Rebecca's call from that phone box on the coast. There was no mobile signal down there; he'd checked that, it had been part of the reason they'd settled on that cottage so Lee Sung couldn't use his contacts to get her location using phone masts.

Now Eddie wouldn't get a chance to speak to her until next day.

He approached his car with caution, aware that the Triad could have trailed him north. He could see no one hidden in the back seat and the muddy state of the reddish soil discouraged him from lying down to feel around the chassis for lumps of explosive.

As he revved the engine, he considered how much longer he could continue without telling the police everything. It was clear the Triad were involved in Grimond's death; they'd sent Eddie his tongue and eyes, but how had Grimond become entangled with them?

And what about Tiny? It looked like they'd done him too. Rebecca said scalping was a speciality. But why Tiny? The big man wasn't smart enough to be in on a con of any sophistication.

They had got onto everything so fast. How were they doing that? Did they have someone in the police giving them information? Were they tracking people electronically? He'd be crazy to drive to Laura's now, to go anywhere near Kim, at least until he knew more about the fallout from today's race, about how these guys operated?

He switched his phone on to call Laura. A voicemail waited, from Rebecca: "Eddie, I'm sorry, I know you said not to ring your mobile but I'm so worried that you didn't answer at the callbox at seven. Is everything all right? I need to speak to you, to hear your voice. I'm going to ring your mobile every hour until I get you. I love you."

Eddie looked at the phone as though she would somehow come out of it and appear in person. He played the message twice more. At least she was okay. He checked his watch; she was due to call again in twenty minutes.

He rang Laura. 'Eddie? So they didn't lock you up and throw away the key?'

'Not yet.' He told her about the interview, then asked about Kim.

'He's driving me crazy watching replays of the King George. He was still shouting you on the twentieth time he watched it.'

'I love that boy already, you know.'

'He's an easy boy to love.'

'It's times like this I wish I'd been a bus driver, Laura.'

'Even you couldn't get a bus over a fence, Eddie. Through one, maybe…you'd never have been happy doing anything but what you're doing now. Things will sort themselves out. Don't worry.'

'You've been a real friend to me.'

'And you to me.'

'I wish things were…simpler.'

'Mmmm.'

He told her of his concerns about being tracked somehow, his fears of leading them to Kim.

'Eddie, he can stay with me as long as you want. As long as he wants. If you think he's going to be safer here…you can talk to him on the phone every day.'

'I don't even think that's a good idea, Laura. I think I need to speak to Campbell Ogilvie and to Mac and maybe even to the police again and try and work something out. I promised Ben Turco I'd protect him, but I'm going to have to call that deal off. Kim's safety's more important than keeping Turco out of jail.'

'Once you've explained that to Turco, he'll understand, I'm sure. Why don't you call him?'

'I don't have a number. I'll need to do some digging. I know Walter, one of his helpers is in Majorca. I might try and get in touch with him for Ben's details.' He checked his watch, anxious about Rebecca's call. He agreed with Laura that they'd have no mobile phone contact for the next few days, that they'd talk on the phone using only public callboxes at pre-arranged times. He gave her the number of the callbox nearest his flat, the one he'd given Rebecca. 'I'm at Newbury tomorrow. I'll be back for six if you can call me then?'

'I will. Stay safe.'

'You too, Laura.'

He hung up. 7.56. The next four minutes passed very slowly. When Rebecca's call came, his screen said "number withheld".

'Eddie?'

'Rebecca! Are you all right?'

'I'm fine, Eddie. It's so good to hear your voice again!'

'And yours. I've missed you.'

'Me too. You were brilliant today on Prince Simba. I'm so proud of you. So proud!'

'I was lucky, in the end.'

'Luck nothing! You were fantastic! Kim must have been over the moon. How is he?'

'Er, over the moon, I suppose. He's staying at Laura's. I haven't seen him since this morning.'

Eddie told her everything about the day. When she heard that Kim was going to be with Laura for a while, Rebecca gave Eddie the silent treatment.

In the darkness, he smiled. 'You're jealous of Laura, aren't you?'

'For what? Are you joking? She's big and fat and goes around smiling or crying all the time. Or hugging people and kissing them!'

Eddie laughed.

'It's not funny!'

'Okay, okay. You're just going over the top, that's all. I think Laura's quite pretty.'

'Oh, do you now! Well why don't you just go and ring her up and talk to her instead of me!'

He laughed again, a little nervously. 'Come on, Rebecca, I'm kidding. Anyway, I told her I won't speak to her until all this is sorted out. We won't have any contact at all.'

She was silent again for a while then said moodily, 'Don't worry, she'll find some excuse to ring you up.'

'She won't. We've agreed that if there's an emergency we'll contact each other through a third party. There's to be nothing direct. It's safer that way for Kim.'

'Well, we'll wait and see.'

'We will. But never mind Laura, how have you been? How is sunny Devon in the depths of winter?'

'It's a nice change from London, I suppose.'

'Does Annelise like it, and your mother?'

'Mother does but the air is a bit too clean and fresh for Annelise.'

'Are you managing to stay indoors okay while it's daylight?'

'God, yes! But it's really boring, we've hardly moved since we came here.'

'It won't be for long. And it's safest. We can't risk you being seen, especially after today. And listen, we need to stick to the plan of no mobile contact. Call me tomorrow at the number I gave you. Call at seven. If I'm not there for some reason, call on the hour until ten, then leave it.'

'Okay.'

'Is it far from you, that callbox?'

'No. Two minutes in the car.'

'When it rang, it came up number withheld here.'

'Well, that's odd, isn't it? I haven't used public phones for years, maybe that's what they do now.'

'Same here. Maybe you're right. What's the number on it?'

'Emmm, let's see…oh, it's been blotted out, some bloody kid with a black felt pen.'

'I suppose graffiti's about all they've got to do down that way.'

'Little bastards.'

They talked about how much longer they'd need to stay apart and of the likelihood of the Triads having started feuding. Rebecca said she might try and make a few discreet calls to see what was happening and that they'd talk again next day.

Eddie had one more call to make, but feared there might already be a bug in his mobile. He drove to a pub and called Campbell Ogilvie from the public phone then sped north.

FIFTY-EIGHT

They met at Tebay services in the northern lakes. It was after 10pm, but it looked to Eddie as though the solicitor had shaved before coming out, He wore a tweed suit with a waistcoat and tie and Eddie envied his discipline. Eddie pushed coffee and carrot cake across the table. 'Peace offering, for dragging you out so late on Boxing Day. You'll have little enough time with your family. I appreciate you coming'

Ogilvie smiled and delicately broke a small piece of cake with his fingers. 'I'd have thought it would have been a champagne celebration for you tonight, Mister Malloy, after today's success.'

'I'm saving that until we've sorted everything out for Kim and we're all settled. You'll be the first on the party invite list.'

'Good. How is he?'

'He's great. Flourishing.'

'Forgive me, but who is he with while you are travelling tonight?'

'Laura Gilpin. Remember, you met her at the hospital? Kim calls her aunt Laura. I'm on my way there now.'

Ogilvie smiled pleasantly, but asking with his eyes that Eddie state his business.

'Mister Ogilvie, you pulled plenty strings to get that interim court order for us. Those forms I filled in...I left something out. Something that could cause you trouble, professionally, I mean.'

The solicitor looked more serious now. 'Go on.'

'I've got a criminal record.'

'How criminal?'

'Jail criminal.'

Ogilvie looked at the ceiling. It was the first time Eddie had seen him rattled. Ogilvie folded his arms and crossed his legs and looked at Eddie, 'You've been to prison?'

'A long time ago, I was young and stupid.'

'What was the conviction?'

'Malicious wounding. GBH.'

'The sentence?'

'Two years. I did eighteen months.'

'A single victim?'

'A man called Kruger, He ran a horse-doping ring and falsely accused me of being involved. It cost me my riding licence and I was warned off the turf for five years.'

'Was Mister Kruger convicted of doping?'

'No. Scot-free. He walked. I sank. I was champion jockey at twenty-one. He killed my career and pushed me close to suicide.'

'How badly was he hurt?'

'He lived in a big house. I kicked him around most of it. He was out of hospital in two weeks. No long term damage.'

Ogilvie took another piece of cake. 'It's going to be very difficult to formalize this guardianship. Probably impossible.'

'Can we withdraw the application and lodge another one? Marie is going to apply, if you think that's wise.'

'His mother?'

'Yes. We had a long talk about it.'

'You say she is going to apply; does she want Kim now?'

Eddie shifted in his seat. 'She thinks it's for the best, given the circumstances.'

'She's had a change of mind since my conversations with her?'

'Yes.'

'I will need to go and see her.'

'She knows that.'

'She'll need to submit to assessment by Social Services over a fair period. They'll need to be convinced her relationship with Kim, her interactions as they call them, are in his best long-term interests.'

'She'll do everything she needs to do.'

'And assuming it's approved, you'll still maintain a relationship with Kim?'

'A close one. A very close one. He's a Malloy. He deserves every chance in life and that's what he's going to get. I just want everything to be done properly from the start. I don't want us constantly looking over our shoulders.'

'Good. He seemed very attached to you by the time he left hospital.'

'We're very close. Good friends. The boy's a genius.'

Ogilvie smiled and took a bigger piece of cake. 'Good. Is there anything else you want to tell me?'

'Only that I'm sorry for lying…on that form. It was stupid.'

'We all do stupid things. Don't be too hard on yourself.'

'Thanks.'

'Give my regards to Kim.'

'I will.'

'I take it he doesn't yet know about this?'

'Not yet.'

'Good luck.'

'Thanks.'

Eddie sat in his car, watching the solicitor drive away through the drifting curtains of rain. He'd expected to feel better with the load off his mind, but he felt worse. The deal with Marie was on the understanding that Kim would move in with Eddie once all the paperwork was done, and that Eddie would never try to talk her into having a relationship with the boy.

That had been an easy trade-off. He wanted Kim with him and he was convinced that as soon as Marie met him, she'd be so taken that she'd relent quickly and want to build some kind of long term future around him.

Anything else you want to tell me? Ogilvie had asked. Eddie slumped in his seat and groaned; what, like a man's eyes and tongue are in a flask in my kitchen? Like the police know I'm withholding information on a crime? My girlfriend has done a deal with a Triad boss to set up mayhem in London's Chinatown? My nephew could yet land in the thick of the whole damned lot of it?

Carrying a brown bag full of groceries, Ben Turco cursed as he made his way through grey slush that had spilled over from the banked up walls of filthy snow thrown sideways by vehicle wheels. He'd forgotten how foul New York winters could be.

Fumbling for his swipe card, he ran it through the reader on the door and gained access to his apartment house. As he made his way toward the elevator, the concierge walked from behind the big walnut desk, his heels sending clicking echoes up through the diaphragm of the building.

'Mr Turco, sir, this came for you 'bout a half hour ago.'

He placed a small package in Turco's left hand, which was still trying to do its share of supporting the shopping. The concierge hit the elevator button and whirring cables responded immediately. Turco thanked the man and rested the brown package on top of the groceries.

Travelling up to his apartment, he stared at the padded bag with the typed address label; nobody knew he lived here. This was the first piece of mail he'd had. Once inside, he went to the kitchen and laid the bag on the long pearl coloured worktop. He opened the package…an audio tape and a typed note on good quality plain paper. It said: 'If you are not back in London by 29th December, a copy of this tape will be sent to the police. When you arrive in London call this number and say who you are. Grimond is dead.'

A central London telephone number was listed. With deepening dread, Turco went to his big black music centre, put the tape in and pressed play. The first voice he heard was his own. The only other one on the tape was Grimond. The conversation was the one they'd had in that motorway service station in Northampton. Incriminating without any doubt.

Turco switched it off. Who had sent this? Grimond must have taped their meeting that day. If they'd got it from Grimond, it seemed a fair bet they'd been the ones who'd attacked him.

And now he was dead.

FIFTY-NINE

As the Boeing 747 carrying Ben Turco made its final approach to Heathrow, it overflew Eddie Malloy's final approach along the A34 to Newbury racecourse. The big jet broke through low cloud and Turco fiddled nervously with his seat belt. He didn't like flying.

As he drove into the racecourse Eddie's mind dwelt on the Triads. He'd spent a peaceful night; no visitors, no crazy phone calls. Perhaps the internal feud was well under way. Maybe Rebecca would have more news in her call this evening. They could then decide when she should come back from Devon.

He wondered how Kim was. The boy would be loving it at Laura's yard, right in with the horses in all that wild wind and open space. The healthy sea air; Eddie found himself filling his lungs as he locked the car and lugged his kitbag toward the Jockeys' Entrance. Clocking on for another day's work. Three rides booked. One man and one boy to keep. And hopefully, in the not too distant future, one very pretty, very brave woman.

After the last race, Eddie was surprised to find a message from Ben Turco asking him to call.

He did. Turco answered on the second ring. 'Eddie! How the hell are you?'

'I'm all right. What brings you back from the Big Apple?'

'That's what I'd quite like to talk to you about, hence the reason I'm on my way to you at the moment.'

'I'm at Newbury races.'

'I know. I should be there in fifteen minutes. Can you wait?'

'Of course, but it's probably best if we meet in the car park.'
Turco put on a camp voice. 'You always were ashamed of
introducing me to your friends!'

Eddie smiled and headed for the car park. Passing the horsebox
area, Eddie saw Matt Nash loading a bay gelding Eddie had ridden
in the third race. He'd pulled the horse up and it occurred to him,
as he watched the lame animal hobble up the ramp, that Matt's luck
had gone on the slide again. He walked over to him. 'Bad?'

Matt sighed and nodded, pointing to the gelding's near hind
fetlock. 'See the swelling?'

'Sorry, Matt. Looks like another one out for the season after
Carpathian. Just as well you've got memories of the King George
to keep you warm.'

'And Cheltenham to look forward to with the Prince.'

'True. Right, I'll leave you to it. Oh, by the way, it wasn't
Rebecca you saw going into that casino that night, it was her sister.
You weren't far off.'

Matt looked at him. 'Who told you that?'

'Rebecca.'

'She hasn't got a sister.'

Eddie smiled. 'Annelise.'

Matt shook his head. 'New one on me. I've known the family
for years. I'm embarrassed to admit I turned down the offer of
being Rebecca's Godfather because I felt I wasn't much more than
a kid myself. I lost touch a bit after her father died, but I'm pretty
sure she ain't got a sister.'

Eddie stared, looking puzzled and troubled. Matt stepped
forward and gripped his arm and smiled, 'She's winding you up,
mate. Or maybe it *was* her that night and she just didn't want you to
think she was out on the town without you.'

'Maybe.'

'Cheer up, they all do it! Women are human too, you know.'

Eddie threaded his way through vehicles, making for his car,
scrolling for Rebecca's number when he heard that Boston accent:
'You'll have an accident doing that.'

He looked up and saw Turco leaning against a silver BMW. He
put away his phone and they shook hands.

Turco said, 'Good to see you still in one piece after another
hard day at the office.'

'Getting injured riding's the least of my worries these days.'

'What's up?'

'You'll have troubles enough of your own, Ben, without listening to mine. What can I do for you?'

'Follow me to some quiet pub and I'll tell you.'

SIXTY

They met again at a country inn. On the drive there, Eddie left a voicemail for Rebecca although he had no idea what he was going to say when she rang.

Eddie watched Turco go to the bar. The Yank was his usual tousled self with his square unshaven jaw and coconut hair. He wore jeans and sneakers and a heavy red and black check lumberjack shirt over a light grey T-shirt.

He came back carrying Budweiser and a whiskey. He sat down and Eddie watched the fire reflect on his round glasses, making his eyes look almost demonically pinpoint.

Turco told him about the tape, and that he hadn't yet called the number they'd given him.

'Are you going to call?'

Turco shrugged. 'Gonna have to.'

Eddie brought him up to date.

'So the cops don't know about the Triads but they do know about Grimond?'

'Yes, but not about you,' Eddie said.

Turco leaned toward the fire, elbows on knees, hands clasped. 'Trouble is, Eddie, how long you gonna be able to keep quiet?'

'Ben, I don't know. Kim has changed everything. I'm happy to take risks for myself, but not with him.'

'That's okay, my friend, I understand. Let's see how things pan out.'

'I know you'll have a plan, Ben, what is it?'

'I'm working on it. I need to figure out what these guys want. It can't be blackmail over this photo-finish scam because they could have blackmailed me just as easy in New York. They want me here to do something for them.'

'Well there's only one way you're going to find out.'

Turco dangled his bottle by the neck and nodded. He rose and went to the telephone in the entrance hallway. Eddie watched him through the glass. Suddenly, Turco signalled him frantically. Eddie joined him as Turco attached a small object to the earpiece of the receiver.

Turco said, 'Sorry, I lost you there. Could you say that again?'

Eddie could hear the angry voice very clearly. 'This is the last time! Tell Mister Malloy he must call soon. I have someone here he'd like to speak to.' Lee Sung laughed. Eddie remembered the laugh, and the voice that had no trace of a Chinese accent.

They returned to the table. Turco finished his beer and looked at Eddie, 'Remember that SiS plan, the one you didn't care for? They want us to try and pull it off.'

'Us?'

'Me and you.'

'Where I get you access to the live broadcast studio?'

'That's the one.'

'How do they know about it?'

'Well I didn't tell 'em.'

Eddie lowered his head, shaking it slowly in despair as he realized he'd told only one other person. He turned to Turco. 'They've caught Rebecca.'

Turco tipped up the bottle, draining the last of the beer. He said, 'They must have been confident of catching her to have their plans so far advanced. They want to do this in four days' time.'

'I spoke to her last night. She was fine. When did you get the message to call them?'

'The package reached me in New York yesterday.'

They looked at each other. Eddie rose from the chair, 'This doesn't add up, Ben. Let me see that number.'

They went to the payphone and Turco attached his speaker. Eddie dialled. One of Lee Sung's henchmen answered and went to get him. Eddie held for over a minute before Lee Sung came on and sarcastically thanked him for returning the call. 'Before we talk business, I have someone who wants to talk to you, Mister Malloy, after which, I think I'll have your full attention.'

Eddie held. Turco, standing close, watched his face intently. Then a very frightened voice came on the line. 'Eddie ... Eddie ...' heavy sobs and Eddie felt himself go weak. 'Eddie ... I'm sorry!'

It was Kim.

SIXTY-ONE

Eddie called Laura. 'Eddie! Is Kim okay?'

'What happened, Laura?' He felt let down, angry.

'What happened? What are you talking about? Rebecca picked him up this morning. Where is he?'

'The Triad got him.'

'Awww, Jesus, no! Awww...' Laura wept and groaned like an animal and that hit Eddie almost as hard as the news about Kim. 'Laura! Laura, Laura! It's okay. It's not your fault. Listen! Look, we'll get him back. I know where he is. It's going to be okay!'

But he couldn't quiet her howls. 'Laura! Please!'

'It's my fault, Eddie! I've never trusted her. I should have called you! Oh Jesus God in heaven!'

'Laura! Laura, listen. I need to know exactly what happened. It's important in getting Kim back. Please believe me, I'm going to get him back. Unharmed. Trust me. Listen. Trust me.'

'Okay, okay!' Laura fought to quell her panic and misery, and Eddie heard her take deep breaths and the howling eased to sobs, sobs and long breaths, then she was able to talk. She told him Rebecca turned up just after nine, alone, smiling, confident, persuasive. She'd told Laura that information she'd gathered in London last night suggested the Triad were close to tracking Kim down. She said she'd told Eddie, who'd asked her to come and pick the boy up. Rebecca said Eddie was afraid his phone had been hacked, that's why he hadn't called Laura direct.

Eddie rang Lee Sung back to fix a meeting. Lee Sung said he would not meet Eddie, only Turco. If Eddie turned up there would be no deal and he would not see the boy again. For all the Chinaman's bluster, Eddie realized that the damage he'd done to Lee Sung that night in London had scared the man; he wasn't willing to risk being in the same room with Eddie.

'Okay, Turco will come and meet you but listen to me ...' Eddie paused to let the Chinaman concentrate, then he spoke slowly and deliberately, 'If you hurt that boy I will kill you. If you hurt that boy I will kill you. I do not want you to be in any doubt that I will kill you if you hurt that boy. No matter what else happens, I will kill you if you hurt that boy.'

Lee Sung laughed but nervousness needs no translation and Eddie realized he'd hit home. He passed the phone to Turco who arranged to meet Lee Sung in London in an hour.

In a daze Eddie returned to his seat. The threat he'd made replayed hypnotically in his head and he realized he'd meant it. If he lost Kim now, he wouldn't want to carry on life in any normal way. He wanted Kim to have a happy adolescence, to have what Eddie had been robbed of.

He'd lost Rebecca, the treacherous Rebecca. No, he hadn't lost her because he'd never had her. She'd had him for an utter fool. A loop of lust through his nose like a ring through an animal's and she'd led him where she wanted.

Even from that first night when she'd called him to London to rescue Matt; when she'd told him a couple of days ago how fierce, how professional the Triads were, he'd thought back to that scene in the basement, which now seemed more like a stage farce.

Rebecca just happening to have a gun in her pocket and being totally cool in producing it. The two bodyguards immediately succumbing and lying on the floor. No doubt Lee Sung suffered more than he'd planned, but that had to have been a setup to get him intimately tied in with Rebecca and committed to Matt and his problems.

And if they were such a vicious crew, so protective of their reputations, why no revenge attempt for the beating Eddie had given Lee Sung?

When Matt needed somewhere to hide and watch Samson's Curls run, Rebecca conveniently organized a friend's flat in Chelsea which Lee Sung's men somehow found very quickly after the race.

Then her sudden departure from Cheltenham that afternoon, supposedly to see her sick mother.

Eddie tried to walk his mind back through the timeline of his conversations with Rebecca. He'd told her about Grimond and the blackmail attempt, which could have resulted in him being warned off. No jockey to manipulate meant no big pay day in the King George, no invitation as a studio guest at SiS. Rebecca told Lee Sung and Lee Sung took care of Grimond.

And then Tiny, another possible witness who might say Eddie had bribed him.

Now Turco gets roped in. Why? Because of Eddie's need to play the big man. Rebecca's skill at pillow talk teased from him all the information about Turco's SiS scam.

Eddie buried his head in his hands. *I thought horses made the biggest fools of people.*

Turco left for London promising he'd call Eddie as soon as he'd met Lee Sung. Eddie rang Peter McCarthy. 'Eddie, tell me this, how come you always manage to call me outside office hours?'

'Just to keep you on your toes, Mac.'

McCarthy recognized the hollowness in Eddie's voice. 'What's wrong, Eddie?'

'I need to see you.'

SIXTY-TWO

By a log fire in a corner of the lounge of the Chequers Hotel in Newbury, McCarthy watched Eddie's face contort as he told the security man what had happened. Eddie finished and looked at the big man with what McCarthy saw as childlike hope.

'I can tell you now, Eddie, you've got no chance unless we bring in some big guns from the Met.'

Eddie stared into his almost empty glass. 'That's what Turco says.'

McCarthy seemed surprised. 'Then he is a clever man.'

Eddie buried his face in his hands, massaged it with his fingers. 'The trouble is they've got Kim, and if the slightest thing goes wrong and these people find out the police are in on it, then I've lost him.'

McCarthy watched him. Over the years, the only strong emotion he'd seen in Eddie was rage. This was fear, despair. Mac leaned forward, reached out and squeezed Eddie's stooped shoulder. It was the first time either could recall any true gesture of comfort between them, and it did something to break through what until now had been a purely professional relationship.

Eddie raised his head and smiled wearily at Mac. And Mac smiled, again with real warmth.

Half an hour later Turco called to say he was on his way back. There'd been no sign of Kim. He'd seen nobody but Lee Sung and his sidekicks. While they waited for Turco, McCarthy worked on building Eddie's commitment for what would have to happen. He told the jockey he had some knowledge of the Triads through a CID friend whose patch in London included Chinatown.

'You have to get these people on the spot, red-handed. You'll never find anyone to testify against them. They've been known to cut a man into small pieces in front of his wife and she will swear she saw nothing. Fear of the Triads is endemic in the Chinese, they're brought up with it the way you were brought up with horses. It's ingrained like a religion. It's unshiftable. It's hundreds of years old.

'The only way to nail them is to catch them mid-crime. That's your sole chance of putting them away. If we can get this Lee Sung, I know the police will appreciate it. And if you get the reputation among the Triads as someone who can get people locked up for a long time, you can be pretty sure they'll find easier targets in future.'

Eddie looked at the big man. 'And if we don't nail them?'

'We'll give them a bloody good scare.'

'Yes, but at what point will you give them the scare, and what will they give Kim?' Eddie could hear the frustration in his own voice and saw that Mac registered it.

McCarthy finally submitted to the heat from the fire, and slid his big coat off to reveal a brown suit Eddie had seen a few times before. Within a minute, Mac had taken his jacket off too.

Quietly he broke back into the subject. 'You know we can't let this go ahead, Eddie? We've got to get them before the show goes on air as such.'

'And how do you plan to do that?'

'We'll have to decide that with the police. There's no way we can put a false result out into every betting shop, you know that. It would finish racing in this country!'

'Not if we handled it properly.'

'Ha! Enlighten me.'

'Wait and talk to Turco. He's the genius.'

'I'm happy to talk turkey with Turco.'

Mac smiled and Eddie found one from somewhere too.

SIXTY-THREE

Turco's eyes gleamed as he came through the door and spotted them in the corner.

Eddie got up and went to meet him, asking anxiously if he'd seen Kim, but Turco hadn't and Eddie, despondent, sat down again. He quietly introduced Turco to Mac, who eyed the American with a degree of caginess he felt ashamed of when he saw how open and friendly Turco was with him.

Turco told them about the meeting. 'They want to do this New Year's Day for several reasons: they're obsessed with some other Triad stealing their idea so they want it done before anyone gets the chance. They've picked Cheltenham as they reckon the market will be strong enough there to stop the bookies realising how much is being placed on one horse. Also, there are seven meetings planned that day, so they're counting on the staff in shops being under too much pressure to pick up on their bets and warn head office in advance.

'And, they want it done in the long distance 'chase because their illegal bookmaking operation will lay the odds-on favourite at odds against.'

Eddie said, 'Well what good will that do them? The horse might win anyway and the proper result would be up within a few minutes. However you manage to manipulate the live pictures, there are betting shops on the track at Cheltenham taking the SiS service. Punters there will know right away that the result is false.

They only need to walk out and see the horses crossing the line live.'

'Ah, but they've thought of that. They're going to have someone cut all telecommunications to Cheltenham just before the off, and that includes slicing the satellite cables at the course.'

'So? It might take a couple of hours to fix, then everyone will know the true result.'

Turco shrugged. 'So what? They'll be long gone with the cash by then!'

Mac spoke for the first time. 'Why did they tell you all this?'

'I don't know. I got the impression they were showing off a bit. And maybe they wanted me to know they'd gone into it in depth so we'd be put off pulling any tricks.'

Eddie said, 'What about Kim, didn't they say anything about where they were holding him?'

Turco shook his head. 'They said they'd hand him over at a pre-agreed point once the result was in and bets paid.'

'Which pre-agreed point?'

'To be confirmed.'

Eddie and Turco looked at each other. McCarthy said, 'Listen, you cannot go ahead with this. I don't care what your plans are to try and retrieve the situation afterwards, but you cannot put out a completely false result!'

'Wait until you hear the retrieval plans first. Tell him, Ben.'

Turco's striking round eyes grew even brighter. When he finished Mac looked at him for a while, wondering at his brain and his imagination. Mac said, 'And you've got all the kit you need here in London to do this?'

'It's being shipped today.'

McCarthy shook his head in wonder. He didn't know how he'd keep Turco out of trouble with Jockey Club officials and the police, and he respected the American for not asking him to. But he'd try to do something if Turco could pull this off.

Mac told them he'd contact his man at Scotland Yard and set up a meeting for tomorrow.

When he'd gone, Turco said to Eddie, 'If you need a bed for the night you're welcome to come and stay at my place.'

Eddie shook his head. 'I want you to show me where your meeting with Lee Sung was. That's where I'll be staying the night.'

'I doubt it,' said Turco, 'We met in a car park.'

Turco could see that Eddie wasn't sure if he was joking. 'No kidding, Eddie. Come home with me. We'll be close to McCarthy's man then if he can set a meeting up tomorrow.' Eddie nodded, too weary to argue.

Eddie's phone rang as he drank tea and watched Turco do marvellous things with his spacewars game on the penthouse window high above the London traffic.

He recognized Laura's voice and realized he was glad to hear it.

'Are you all right?' she asked.

'I'm okay. I'm sorry, I should have called you back, Laura. How are you?'

'Calmer. I'm sorry about earlier.'

'Don't apologize. I felt for you. I'm sorry I couldn't be there to offer some comfort, God knows I owe you plenty.'

'You owe me nothing. No tit for tat, remember? Friends don't trade things off.'

'I know, but, well, oh, you know.'

'I know, I know.'

'Good! We all know.'

They laughed.

'Any word?' Laura asked.

'Yes, but no good news. Something's been arranged but it's best not to talk about it on mobiles. Where are you?'

There was a slight hesitation, then she said, 'Outside your flat.'

He didn't speak.

'I felt terrible, Eddie. I had to see you. I wanted to see you.' She waited, uncertain.

'Can you drive to London?'

'I can drive to hell and back.'

He smiled. 'That's corny, Laura.'

'It was, wasn't it? I promise never to be corny again.'

'I'll hold you to it.'

Eddie gave her directions. Before saying goodbye she said, 'Eddie, listen, Kim's going to be all right, I can sense it. I know he will be.'

'I hope so.'

'He will. Keep your chin up. I'll see you soon.'

SIXTY-FOUR

Laura, Eddie and Ben all left the penthouse at 9.45 next morning, Sunday, 29 December. The weather forecast held no threats of abandonments; the seven New Year's Day meetings looked certain to go ahead.

They took a cab across to Scotland Yard to meet McCarthy and his contact. McCarthy introduced him: Chief Inspector Mills. He was a big man, early fifties maybe, with a salt and pepper moustache and an upright bearing. Eddie had noticed that about a number of senior policemen he'd met over the years; they carried themselves well, had a definite presence, though in Mills's case his six foot three, fifteen stone frame, gave him a good start.

Eddie introduced Laura to McCarthy as well as to Mills. The Chief Inspector led them into a meeting room. The strong smell of brewing coffee brought a smile to Turco's face, which, for once, was clean shaven.

They talked for almost two hours. Mills made Turco go over his plan again and again and by the end they were confident they'd covered most eventualities. Next stop was a hotel near Marble Arch for a meeting with the MD of SiS. Turco wanted to have it at the SiS studio, but the others thought that wouldn't be such a good idea in case Lee Sung's men were watching the place.

The only other meeting planned for that day was one Turco had to attend that evening, at an address to be advised by Lee Sung, who wanted a live demonstration of the image manipulation.

But Chief Inspector Mills suggested Turco put Lee Sung off until the night before, New Year's Eve. None of them knew how Lee Sung would react and while a postponement wasn't crucial to their plans they agreed it would give them a greater chance of success.

Turco called the number Lee Sung had given him, which Mills had identified as being a callbox in a hotel near Wardour Street.

Lee Sung seemed suspicious when Turco told him he couldn't make it but the American played his part brilliantly. 'Hey, listen, I can bring the stuff, no problem, but I'm telling you it won't work properly yet. You want to see a demo on video and on live TV and it's got to be adjusted for that. If you're happy seeing it not working properly then I'll bring it right along tonight. Just say the word.'

But Lee Sung conceded that Tuesday 31st would be okay, warning him that if the equipment didn't work to his satisfaction the deal was off and the boy would be killed. Turco did not tell anyone about this final threat.

Turco spent the remainder of that day and most of the next playing his games. McCarthy went home. Eddie and Laura went walking in London.

To Eddie that Monday seemed the longest day. At least on Tuesday they'd have the tension of waiting for Turco returning from his demo to Lee Sung. That was where the first part of the plan would be put in place. If that failed, things would be much tougher.

When Turco made the call late on Tuesday afternoon, he was given the address and warned to travel alone. Eddie and Laura helped plot his route then packed his gear into the rented BMW. They stood close together watching the tail lights disappear.

The house was in East London, well outside Lee Sung's normal area, but that didn't bother Turco or the others too much. They knew it would probably be a one-off visit for the Chinaman too.

It was a bungalow on a sprawling estate, and it took Turco a while to find it. The rain fell gently as he walked up the path. One of Lee Sung's sidekicks opened the door then his friend joined him and they helped Turco bring in his kit.

Lee Sung waited inside. He grunted at the American and pointed to the big TV set, which had been wheeled into the middle of the room. Turco could see the castor indentations in the carpet in the corner. He walked around the set as though assessing an accident victim, looked suitably pensive, well aware that the three men were watching him closely. He signalled the two younger men to bring his three leather bags over beside the set.

Turco knelt down behind the TV and opened his bags taking out three separate cream-coloured units plus a keyboard, cabling and two remote control pads. A smaller bag contained a toolkit and Turco opened it. From the other bag he took an electrical extension and held it up toward one of the men without speaking or looking. The man hurried to plug it in a socket on the longest wall.

Turco said to him, 'I need you to stay there by that switch and turn it on and off as I tell you.' The man nodded. Turco took a screwdriver and removed the panel at the back of the TV and started unrolling his cables. Lee Sung moved closer.

Turco worked silently for five minutes, rigging up various things, telling the man by the socket to switch on and off now and again. All the time Lee Sung inched closer.

Turco knelt. He straightened his back and turned toward the other young man. 'I need more light. Find me a flashlight or something.'

The man looked baffled. Turco held out his arm, clicking his thumb back and forward. 'Flashlight, you know? Torch?'

Lee Sung barked something and the man hurried away. Turco made to look at his watch and saw he hadn't one. 'Shit!' He looked at Lee Sung , so close now he could smell him. 'You got a watch on?' Lee Sung quickly held his wrist toward Turco, who put his hand out. 'Gimme it a minute.'

Lee Sung slid a heavy silver watch off his wrist and handed it to Turco. Turco raised it and looked closely at the dial, screwing up his eyes. Then he leant forward to make a tiny adjustment to one of the units. Again he leant back, again he narrowed his eyes. 'Where's that goddamn light!' He looked impatiently at Lee Sung. 'Go see where he's got to with that light, will ya? How the hell's a man supposed to work without light?'

Lee Sung obeyed.

Turco was singing when he got back to the flat. His voice was less than tuneful, but as Laura and Eddie heard it carry along the hallway they felt a surge of relief. They talked for a long time; Turco, high because of what he'd done, the others too tense to sleep. They even tried Turco's spacewars game but nothing could take their minds off the fact that tomorrow was D-Day. Make or break.

SIXTY-FIVE

The Cheltenham race was timed at 2.10. Turco's target was a horse called Grasshopper Green, which would start at a minimum price of 20-1 according to the papers. Some forecast 33-1.

Lee Sung had more than a thousand men in place all over the capital. He'd thought of trying to cover more of the country, but in London a strange face in a betting shop was far from unusual, and big bets were often accepted without suspicion.

Of the 3,000 shops in the London area, Lee Sung had done his homework. He knew which were frequented by Chinese, well known in the betting world as fearless gamblers. A Chinese man placing a £250 bet on a 33-1 chance wasn't unheard of.

Each agent held £250 to put on the horse, which, even if it started at the minimum forecast odds, would return over £5 million for Lee Sung. None of the agents would find out the selection until five minutes before the off time.

Lee Sung had been impressed when Turco suggested they communicate the chosen horse by using its saddlecloth number. He told Lee Sung he could easily arrange to have the second hand of the on-screen clock stop at 2.05 07 signifying the number 7 to the agents.

Then the bets would be placed a few minutes before the off. Too late to alert anyone or shorten the price at the track, even if the communications sabotage at Cheltenham went wrong.

At exactly 2.10 Rebecca would have Kim with her on the centre of Tower Bridge. Eddie was sending a woman to pick him up but he'd been told the boy would not be handed over until the result was called and confirmed. If anything went wrong, Lee Sung had warned that the drop into the Thames from Tower Bridge was a long one.

Turco told the Chinaman that Eddie had arranged an SiS studio visit for three people, scheduled for 1.15. He promised that would give him plenty time to set things up, reassuring Lee Sung that the kit wouldn't need all the tweaking he'd had to do for the demo. He told Lee Sung that if Kim wasn't handed over straight after the result, that Eddie himself would go live on air from the studio to warn all betting shops not to pay out.

Lee Sung told him to pick up his man outside Moorfields Eye Hospital at exactly one o'clock.

And they did. Eddie and Turco looking suitably tense as the black-suited Chinaman in the white shirt and black tie got in the back. It was a trip of only a few hundred yards to Corsham Street and SiS headquarters.

Eddie got them in and past security, then downstairs to the basement studio where he introduced Turco and the Chinaman as friends. The studio manager and his staff had been briefed. They'd thought they might find it tough shamming fright and surprise when the Chinaman pulled the gun, but they had no difficulty.

Turco faced the real acting job now, trying to reassure everyone that all would be well if nobody did anything silly. Eddie took a backseat as the American, loving the limelight, the drama, moved hurriedly but calmly around, running cables, tinkering with the edit suite, all the time making comforting noises.

'Now, take it easy, guys. We didn't want to do this. We're victims of these crazy people same as you are. Bigger victims. But don't worry. Stay cool. This guy will be outta here by 2.20. Just a little matter of a horserace to fix first. In the meantime you'd best go about your business of providing a normal service to all them friendly bookmakers out there.'

And the SiS team did that; cueing video tape, mixing in text shows, giving commentaries and watching the clock as it moved toward 2.10.

At 1.50 Laura Gilpin sat in Eddie's Audi in the car park of the Tower Hotel on the north bank of the Thames at Tower Bridge. She could see most of the bridge. The day was clear with a stiff breeze coming down the river. There was no sign of Rebecca and Kim.

At four minutes past two, the blonde woman appeared, walking toward the centre of the bridge from the south bank. That looked like Kim with her. He wore a long coat that Laura knew didn't belong to him. Rebecca's coat was wide with long loose sleeves, and although the boy appeared to be holding her hand, Laura thought he might be tied to Rebecca's wrist.

She locked the car and moved toward the bridge.

At 2.05 and 07 seconds, the clock on SiS screens stopped for five seconds and 1,017 Chinese agents, each in a different shop, filled in the name Grasshopper Green on betting slips, which already had the £250 stake written on. They moved toward the cashiers.

In the darkened SiS studio, the one showing most tension was the black-suited Triad man in the corner. He held the gun at eye-level and his arms ached. He'd been sweating heavily for the past ten minutes and his acrid smell filled the room.

The mischievous Turco kept screwing up his nose and staring at the man. Turco sat at the controls of the big edit suite and the studio commentator was set to take over from the on-course broadcaster at Cheltenham, whose reception from the studio was about to be cut anyway.

The horses moved into line at the start. Turco stayed cool. This wouldn't be hard for him. All he had to control was one horse; it didn't matter a damn where the others ran, as long as he moved the image of Grasshopper Green forward at the right time.

On Tower Bridge, Rebecca watched the fat woman walk toward her and she gripped Kim's hand tighter. In her left hand was a phone that she held to her ear. On the other end of it, in a London betting shop Lee Sung watched the field for the 2.10 come under starter's orders.

As agreed, Laura stayed at least a hundred yards away, though she could see Kim smiling and nodding bravely, trying to reassure her. Laura's phone rang.

'Is Kim there?'

'He's here, Eddie. He looks fine.'

'Is it Rebecca who's with him?'

'Yes.'

'Is she holding him?'

'Yes.'

'Is he close to the parapet? Is he in danger?'

'He's close but his feet are firmly planted on the ground. He'll be okay. I won't let her do anything to him.' Laura's eyes hadn't left Rebecca since she'd stopped on the centre of the bridge.

'Don't go closer until the race is over,' Eddie said.

'I won't, Eddie, don't worry.'

At Cheltenham the starter dropped the flag and the field set off over four miles on soft ground, a journey that would take around eleven minutes. Suddenly, the service to the on-course betting shops blacked out and all landline telephones went dead. People hurried out of the racecourse betting shops to watch the race live.

Lee Sung stood at the rear of the big betting shop in a London suburb. His smile widened as he watched Grasshopper Green's steady progress past rivals. Turco played the dramatist all the way to the end, manipulating the image to come late on the run in and win by a length.

Back live at Cheltenham, the real Grasshopper Green struggled over the last in fifth place.

Lee Sung grinned wide as he watched an SP of 33-1 flash up on the screen. If all 1,017 agents had placed their bets as planned, the bookies would be paying out more than eight and a half million pounds. He asked Rebecca to repeat herself because he hadn't been listening.

'Is everything all right? Can I let the boy go?'

Lee Sung nodded, still smiling. 'Everything fine. Let him go.'

In the SiS studio the gunman backed toward the door, then realized he was supposed to get the key from the studio manager to lock them in. Rushing at the man he demanded the key. He backed away again through the door and as he was locking it, he heard a voice warning him to keep completely still. Turning slowly, he saw four armed policemen in bullet-proof clothing aiming guns at him.

Lee Sung stood, dazed by his success. He would be recognized by his contemporaries now as a great man, a brilliant Triad leader. Pulling the betting slip from his pocket he walked toward the pay-out counter. The manager asked him if he would mind waiting until the jockeys had weighed in and would he accept a cheque for £5,000 and the balance in cash.

'No cheque! Cash!' he shouted loudly.

'But...'

'No cheque! Cash!'

The manager said, 'Okay, sir. Hold on a minute, I'll see if someone can help us out.' He went through a door in the rear of the shop and returned almost immediately, followed by two smiling plain-clothes policemen.

Confusion replaced anger on Lee Sung's face and he turned quickly, trying to leave, only to find the two men 'queuing' behind him smiling and gripping his arms.

In 1,017 other London betting shops the Chinese agents stood staring in dismay at losing betting slips. They couldn't understand why this great horse ran such a bad race when they'd been promised a good percentage. He'd barely managed to finish the course, never mind win.

On Tower Bridge, Rebecca watched warily as the big woman came toward her. Slipping the mobile phone back into her pocket, Rebecca carefully unlocked the handcuffs from Kim's wrist.

She looked around. There were few people on the bridge, none close by. Except Laura. She stopped in front of them now and Kim wriggled free and went to her side. Laura put an arm across his shoulder.

Behind Rebecca, Laura watched two plain-clothes men approaching as arranged, and if things were working out, Rebecca would be looking at two more coming from the north bank. But Rebecca stared at Laura, almost haughtily. Then her look suddenly softened and for a moment Laura thought she might apologize. But she didn't, she started walking away.

Laura said quietly, 'Rebecca ...' and as she turned her blonde head Laura hit her square on the chin with a straight-armed fist.

SIXTY-SIX

By 6pm, Turco had a party going in his flat, and the high tech SiS boys loved his spacewars game. McCarthy and Chief Inspector Mills were in good form, with Mac the most relaxed Eddie had ever seen him.

Since he'd got Kim back, Eddie wouldn't let him outside touching distance. Laura stayed just as close to both of them and all three now sat on the big couch while Eddie told Kim how they'd pulled it off.

'It was mostly down to Ben. When he did the demo for Lee Sung he planted a microchip in his watch that not only told us exactly where the guy was at every minute of the day, it also recorded his conversations. The tape alone should be enough to put him away for twenty years, never mind Grimond's murder, your kidnapping and the attempted fraud.

'As soon as we knew which betting shop Lee Sung was in, it only took minutes for the SiS signal decoder in that shop to be identified and isolated, so it was only that one shop that got the false race. All the others were kept live for a prearranged stopping of the clock that would indicate which horse they should be putting Lee Sung's cash on. Then they were switched back to the proper service. So all the Triad stake money went down the drain. McCarthy and Mister Mills set up the police operation, and for once everything went sweet as a nut.'

He ruffled Kim's hair. 'Remember it this way. You'll find as you go through life that few things will work out so well.'

Laura said to him, 'You sound just like a very serious uncle!'

Eddie smiled. 'I am, aren't I, Kim?'

Kim smiled and said, 'Are we going to Laura's place?'

'Do you want to go?'

'I like your place, but Laura's is my favourite.'

'I thought it might be. I need to ask you something before we go.'

'Something bad?'

'No. Not bad. Just something you'll have to decide about.'

Kim waited. Eddie said, 'While you were at Laura's, I spoke to Marie, my sister, your mother. And I met Mister Ogilvie to talk over a few things.'

Kim watched him.

'Look, it's the first day of a new year. We can stop off on the way to Laura's, stop at Newmarket and meet your mother, and your grandmother. They're waiting.'

'What for?'

'To meet you. To make a new start.'

Kim watched Eddie's face intently. 'Did your sister ask you to bring me. Was it her who suggested the new start?'

Eddie noticed that Kim had called Marie his mother only a handful of times back in the hospital when Eddie was trying to explain things. Since then it had been "your sister". He wouldn't even use her first name. Now Kim had nailed him with a question he hadn't expected. 'No, Kim, she didn't. I raised it with her.'

'Was it my grandmother who made her give me away?'

The boy was stripping down Eddie's romantic vision of how this was all supposed to pan out. 'Partly. She and my father, my late father.'

'If it had been her choice alone, do you think she'd still have made your sister put me up for adoption?'

'You've thought about this a lot, haven't you?'

Kim nodded. Eddie sighed and finger-combed his hair. 'Yes. I think my mother would have forced Marie into having you adopted.'

'I don't think your mother and father treated you very well either, did they?'

Eddie turned to look at Laura. 'Laura didn't tell me anything,' Kim said, 'it's just a feeling I've got about it.'

'A lot of stuff happened back then, Kim. A hell of a lot. I'll tell you about it sometime.'

'When I'm older?'

'When *I'm* older. I'm already thinking you're more mature than I am now, never mind when I was twelve.'

Kim smiled.

'Well, what's it to be? Straight to Alnwick or a stop-off in Newmarket on this first of January?'

'Do *you* want me to go and meet them?'

'I want you to do what you want to do.'

'I don't want you to feel bad.'

Eddie found it hard to resist ruffling the boy's hair, or hugging him. 'I won't feel bad. I promise. I'll be happy whatever you decide.'

'I'd like the new start to be at Laura's, with you and her, That's where I'd like to get to before midnight so we can all finish the first of January there, by the sea, with the horses. I might go to Newmarket someday, but not today.'

Eddie reached to the table beside him and picked up his champagne glass. He passed a glass to Laura and orange juice to Kim and raised his in a toast: 'Non-stop to Alnwick. All aboard!'

SIXTY-SEVEN

Kim was asleep in the back when they reached Alnwick, and between them they carried him carefully into the house and put him to bed. Eddie stretched and yawned and put his arm around Laura. She put one around his waist. They turned to each other. He rested his forehead on hers and they looked into each other's eyes, unblinking, for a long time as though locked into something.

'Tired?' Eddie asked.

'Kind of.'

'Bed?'

'Kind of.'

He eased his head back to look at her. 'Kind of?'

'Yes. Kind of'

'Bed's bed.'

'I wanted this bed to be in a special place.'

'What, like the kitchen?'

'Ha ha.'

'Take me to this special place,' he said, yawning and loosening his tie.

'Okay but I wouldn't start getting undressed. Not just yet.'

Laura opened a huge airing cupboard at the foot of the stairs and pulled out heaps of blankets, piling them into Eddie's arms.

'What the hell are we doing, sleeping on the floor or something?'

'Worse than that.' She kept dragging them out until she too held a stack.

'Come on,' she said and Eddie followed her through the kitchen, shaking his head.

She led him outside, then locked the door. 'We'll be gone a couple of hours. Kim'll be safe.'

'Laura! Where are we going?'

'To the special place.'

'It's bloody freezing! If you think I'm making love in a barn or something … !'

'Worse than that.' She was walking away from the house now.

'Laura, for God's sake!'

'Oh stop moaning! You big cry baby. Come on.'

'Where are we going, you crazy woman?'

'The beach.'

'You're kidding! Tell me you're kidding!'

'No kidding. Hurry up or we'll be late.'

Eddie smiled through his shivers and plodded on with his armful of blankets.

He refused to strip until he was under every blanket; the weight of them made undressing almost impossible. But they managed it and they lay in each other's arms on the beach listening to the wind and the sea and watching the diamond sharp stars.

Eddie said, 'How long have you been planning this?'

'Since the first time we were on the beach, walking the horses in the sea, remember?'

He smiled. 'A lot of water under the bridge since then.'

'A lot of water under the britches too.'

He smiled again then kissed her and gradually the sensation of cold and of dark and of vastness narrowed into the tiniest of worlds.

They lay still, side by side, holding hands, watching the dark sky. Warm now, Laura said, 'I'm hungry. Couldn't you just murder a Chinese?'

'Is this as good as the jokes get? Who writes your stuff?'

'All my own work. Wanna hear some more?'

'Later. Let's go and find a normal bed. An uncrazy bed. A bed we can sleep in.'

'We need to swim first.'

'No chance!'

'You mean fat chance. Freeze there or freeze here!' and Laura rolled away from him dragging the blankets. Grabbing as many as she could she set off running toward the sea swirling them behind her.

'Laura! Jeez, I'm freezing!'

Her whoops came to him on the cold wind and, naked, he raced after her following her deep footprints in the sand. She let the blankets go and one flew either side of him as he caught her knee-deep in the icy surf. They fell screaming in shock and joy and revelation as the ocean opened and with it, the world.

Dear Reader,

Thanks for buying *The Third Degree*. The next Eddie Malloy novel, *Dead Ringer*, will be published in February 2014.

Best wishes
Richard and Joe

13747365R00133

Printed in Great Britain
by Amazon.co.uk, Ltd.,
Marston Gate.